T5-AQQ-212

"I think I'll have a filet mignon. And a really, really big baked potato with all the trimmings," Ally said.

"Only a filet mignon?" Danny asked. "I thought you were hungry enough to eat a horse."

Ally made a shocked face. "I could never eat Black Beauty."

Danny had to laugh. "I was speaking figuratively, and you know it. Of course, you're making up for it with the loaded potato."

The dining room was crowded and Ally lowered her voice, looking at him conspiratorially. "Humor me. I'm pregnant. I get strange cravings, and I can't tell from one day to the next what they will be for."

Danny just smiled and signaled for the waiter. He knew all about cravings. In his case, though, they were not for food.

Dear Reader,

Sometimes military life leads a man or a woman in a direction he or she hadn't originally intended. Both air force TSGT Danny Murphey and Ally Carter thought they knew exactly where they were going. Then life intruded.

Danny was baseball, apple pie, mom and family. He wanted a home and a family, and he fully expected to be responsible for taking care of them. When he met independent Ally Carter, he thought he'd found the perfect woman. Ally Carter had a mind of her own. She'd come from a less traditional family. Her father had been a cultural anthropologist studying in the Middle East when he met her mother, a native of Tamalya. In Ally's rebellion against her mother's traditional upbringing, she almost lost her own happiness.

How do you make two diametrically opposed personalities come together in a meeting of minds (and bodies)? You throw in an unexpected pregnancy, assignment to a Middle Eastern war zone, and mix well. The result is lasting love.

Though there are military special operations schools that prepare servicemen and women for their assignments, I have left the details purposely vague, and I have invented the foreign country in question. However, the reactions and emotions of our characters are real.

I hope you come to know and understand Danny and Ally as I do. And I hope you enjoy reading their story.

Fondly,

Bonnie Gardner

THE SERGEANT'S BABY
Bonnie Gardner

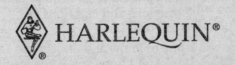

TORONTO • NEW YORK • LONDON
AMSTERDAM • PARIS • SYDNEY • HAMBURG
STOCKHOLM • ATHENS • TOKYO • MILAN • MADRID
PRAGUE • WARSAW • BUDAPEST • AUCKLAND

If you purchased this book without a cover you should be aware
that this book is stolen property. It was reported as "unsold and
destroyed" to the publisher, and neither the author nor the
publisher has received any payment for this "stripped book."

ISBN 0-373-75071-4

THE SERGEANT'S BABY

Copyright © 2005 by Bonnie Gardner.

All rights reserved. Except for use in any review, the reproduction or
utilization of this work in whole or in part in any form by any electronic,
mechanical or other means, now known or hereafter invented, including
xerography, photocopying and recording, or in any information storage
or retrieval system, is forbidden without the written permission of the
publisher, Harlequin Enterprises Limited, 225 Duncan Mill Road,
Don Mills, Ontario M3B 3K9, Canada.

All characters in this book have no existence outside the imagination of
the author and have no relation whatsoever to anyone bearing the same
name or names. They are not even distantly inspired by any individual
known or unknown to the author, and all incidents are pure invention.

This edition published by arrangement with Harlequin Books S.A.

® and TM are trademarks of the publisher. Trademarks indicated with
® are registered in the United States Patent and Trademark Office, the
Canadian Trade Marks Office and in other countries.

www.eHarlequin.com

Printed in U.S.A.

In loving memory of my dad, George W. Purcell, Major,
U.S. Army Ret. (March 19, 1925–February 17, 2004).
He was my first military hero.

To Mud, as always.

As always, I thank, for their hard work and dedication,
the military men and women who sacrifice so much to
keep our world safe, and the families they must
leave behind to keep the home fires burning.

Books by Bonnie Gardner

HARLEQUIN AMERICAN ROMANCE
911—SGT. BILLY'S BRIDE
958—THE SERGEANT'S SECRET SON
970—PRICELESS MARRIAGE
1019—SERGEANT DARLING
1067—THE SERGEANT'S BABY

Don't miss any of our special offers. Write to us at the
following address for information on our newest releases.

Harlequin Reader Service
U.S.: 3010 Walden Ave., P.O. Box 1325, Buffalo, NY 14269
Canadian: P.O. Box 609, Fort Erie, Ont. L2A 5X3

Prologue

Two Years Ago
Fort Walton Beach, Florida

Allison Carter stood in her bra and panties in front of the closet and tried to decide what to put on. She'd always preferred slimming blacks and dark colors, but tonight she and her fiancé, Danny Murphey, were going to announce their engagement at Danny's air-force unit's annual Fourth of July bash on the beach. She needed something that shouted celebration, for the nation's birthday *and* her own special day.

"I like the red one," Danny said from behind her. He wrapped his arms around hers, pinning them to her sides, and drew her to him. He nuzzled her neck, his breath warm and arousing against her cheek. He was referring to the crimson silk sheath with the oriental motif.

Ally had to admit that she looked great in that dress when she was wearing four-inch heels, but on the sandy beach, they would be very much out of place, nor would she be able to walk. Plus, considering her five-foot frame, she wasn't so sure the dress would have the same effect when she had on flat sandals.

Ally turned around and found Danny's lips. She tasted him hungrily, and soon she wasn't worrying about what to wear.

What was there about this man that made him different from the others she'd dated? Ally wondered with delight. She felt Danny harden against her, but she gently pushed him away.

"There's plenty of time for that later, Danny," she said breathlessly, turning back to the open closet. "Tonight's important. Tonight, we'll officially be a couple."

"We aren't now?" Danny countered. "We've been all but living together for months. It's hardly a secret."

"I know," Ally replied. "But it's a big deal for a woman. I can't wait to introduce you to the people I work with," she said as she selected a fuchsia sundress. She'd always thought it a little bright, but Danny had helped her pick it out. And she could wear sandals with it. "Will this one pass inspection?"

"Definitely."

Danny reached around her and grabbed a moss-green polo shirt. Ally loved the way it stretched across his broad chest and over his wide shoulders. She smiled as she thought of the day she'd helped him pick it out. Telling her that he wore green almost every day, he'd rejected it almost immediately. She'd had to explain to him that with his tanned complexion, Irish green eyes and red hair it was perfect, and nowhere close to the same green as his battle-dress air force uniform. She chuckled, remembering.

"I don't know why it matters, anyway," Danny said.

"What matters?"

"Introducing me to your friends from work."

"Not friends, Danny. *Colleagues,*" she corrected him. "My work is important to me. So are the people I work with."

"Yeah, but you'll be quitting soon enough," Danny said.

Had he really just said that? Ally turned, her hands on her hips, and stared at him. Surely he was joking. But his expression proved that he was serious. "Why on earth would I be quitting my job?"

"No Murphey has ever allowed his wife to work. Not while he was alive, anyway," Danny said.

"Allowed his wife to work? *Allowed?*" Ally repeated with incredulity. "What gives you Murphey men or any other men, for that matter, any say in the matter?"

He gaped at her as though she'd spoken in tongues. "As the head of the family," he said slowly, as if addressing a slow child, "it's the duty of the man of the house to provide for his wife and children."

"I did not spend four years in college and work my buns off getting myself established in government civil service to have you or any man tell me that I can't work, Danny!" Ally exclaimed.

He shrugged. "Okay. Let's drop it for now. We have a party to go to. Let's have fun." He smiled and kissed Ally on the top of her head, then finished dressing. "We can hash the working thing out tomorrow."

Chapter One

Fayetteville, North Carolina

Allison Carter smoothed her tailored business suit over her rounding belly and drew in a deep breath. She hadn't realized how difficult it would be to work in her condition, but she'd made her bed—literally— and now she had to lie in it. At least now in her new position as instructor in this specialty school, her life had taken "normal" parameters. Her exhausting travel schedule had been reduced so as to be nearly nonexistent.

As a woman of Middle-Eastern descent and an instructor at the Military Deployment Readiness School, she'd been busy training service members for the culture shock they would encounter when they arrived at their posts in the Middle East. Her days off had been few, given the current state of world affairs, but she was happy that she had settled into her present job.

She had already been a civil service employee, so

when the bulletins seeking instructors with expertise about that part of the world had been posted, she had eagerly submitted her résumé. With her background, she'd readily gained the appointment. The opportunity couldn't have come at a better time. She'd just been through a bitter breakup with the man she'd hoped to marry, and she'd appreciated the opportunity to move far away from him.

Though much of Ally's knowledge of the Middle East had come because her mother had come from Tamahlya, a neighboring country to Tamahlyastan, the site of the current unpleasantness, the customs and traditions were so similar that they were nearly interchangeable. Ally had also taken courses in college on the subject. Little had she known then that the things she had learned from her mother and her esoteric college minor would ever be put to such good use.

She truly enjoyed preparing military and civilian personnel to take assignments in a part of the world where the lifestyles and traditions were completely alien to them. True, most of the men and women she taught already knew a lot about the restrictions in Middle Eastern society, but she was also able to explain and illustrate using her mother's experiences.

To know that her students were well prepared for their foreign assignments was very satisfying. Thanks to her classes, they would be less likely to make innocent mistakes that could cause anything from a minor misunderstanding, such as using the wrong hand to pick up food, to a major incident like speaking to a woman without permission.

At 0729 hours, she gathered up her notes and her laptop computer and stepped from her office into the adjacent classroom. She was sure that her lesson plans would cover all instances that any of her students would encounter.

There were a few empty seats in the room, but a quick head count confirmed that everyone on her class printout was already present. She called the roll, more to become familiar with the men and women she would be working with than to ensure that they were who they were supposed to be. Attendance was never a problem in this training course.

She was halfway through the list when the classroom door opened.

Colonel Kathryn Palmore, the commander of the Air Force Deployment Readiness School, walked in. "I'm sorry to interrupt you, Ms. Carter," she said, "but we have a few last-minute additions to your class."

Allison smiled. She liked Kathryn Palmore and often spent spare moments discussing books, movies—anything but international affairs—with the attractive woman. "Certainly, Colonel," she said. "We have a few extra chairs."

Then her two last-minute students stepped into the room.

Their red berets folded and tucked into the large cargo pockets on the thighs of their camouflage battle-dress uniforms told Allison that they were combat controllers. Their specialized training allowed them to parachute into unfamiliar territory, secure an area and set up air-traffic control operations in advance of incoming aircraft. Such rigorous training made them a cocky group. How familiar she was with that uniform, those men—and one combat controller in particular.

"Sorry to interrupt you, Miz Carter," a familiar voice, laced with sarcasm, said.

Allison looked into Danny Murphey's eyes. His russet hair was cut regulation short as always; his battle-dress uniform was as immaculately pressed as ever. He was the consummate air commando, from his red beret down to the high-laced jump boots.

The anger in his tone, however, was certainly not regulation, and it was impossible to ignore. His Irish eyes were not smiling, and Allison knew why.

Her breath caught and her heart skipped a beat. They may have broken up over two years ago, but she and Danny seemed destined to forever walk in and out of each other's lives. The last time had been just six months ago, and Danny was obviously unhappy about the way she had left him that time.

He would be even less amused if he figured out her secret. Considering her rounded belly, it wouldn't be a matter of *if* but *when*.

Steeling herself for anything, Allison watched as Danny and the other man—someone she didn't know—sauntered confidently into the room. "Have a seat, gentlemen," she said, mustering up a brisk, professional tone. "I'll check your paperwork later. We're just about to get started."

Allison didn't need to read any paperwork to

know the vital statistics for Technical Sergeant Daniel Xavier Murphey. She'd been intimate with every inch of his well-muscled physique, from his hair to his feet. She'd known him almost as well as she knew herself. No, she didn't need to read anything. His eyes used to shine down on her, but that was before he'd issued the ultimatum that had been the beginning of the end.

Colonel Palmore stepped outside, leaving Allison to deal with her students.

Though she had hoped it would take Danny days to notice, Allison saw it the instant Danny realized her condition. His eyes narrowed, and he seemed to hold her against the dry-erase board behind her with his accusing gaze. Allison held her breath and readied herself for the scene she was certain he was going to make.

To his credit, Danny held his tongue, but Allison felt his apparent acceptance, his silence, like the tension of waiting for a time bomb to go off once the button had been pushed. The minutes crawled by. How was she going to get through the rest of the morning, the remainder of the class, anticipating the explosion that was sure to come.

DANNY DIDN'T KNOW how he'd managed to keep it together through that interminable morning, but he had. Now was his chance. He couldn't believe that the woman he'd wanted to spend the rest of his life with had found someone else so quickly—someone who was obviously okay with her working and carrying a baby at the same time.

Ally hadn't changed much since he'd last seen her six months ago. Except for her swelling belly, she was still petite and slim. Her jet-black hair was pinned up in a businesslike manner in deference to her job, but Danny remembered that it shone like black silk and smelled of roses when he pulled out the hairpins and let it tumble loose around her shoulders. How he'd loved to rake his fingers through her long locks.

He shook the image out of his head. No, he couldn't keep thinking of her that way. Ms. Carter—he had to think of her as that—had finally excused the class, giving them a little over an hour to eat at either the base chow hall, the Servicemen's Club or some other nearby eating establishment before class reconvened. Jake Magnussen, the guy who had walked in late with him, had jerked his head for Danny to come on, but Danny waved him off. "I want to ask the instructor something," he had said, and Magnussen went on without him.

Danny was now alone in the room with Allison Carter, the woman who'd been a major player in his dreams for the future. "I guess congratulations are in order," he said slowly, trying mightily to temper his anger and disguise his pain. He hated like hell that Allison—his Ally—might realize just how much her rejection had hurt him.

Ally looked up from busily policing her stuff. Obviously startled by the sound of his voice, she nearly dropped the notes she'd been gathering. "Oh," she squeaked, "I thought I was alone."

"I said," Danny repeated, pausing for effect, "that I thought I needed to congratulate you."

Her expressive, dark eyebrows knitted in consternation above her gray eyes. "For what?"

"Your marriage…so soon after leaving my bed." The Ally he knew might have wanted a career and family, but he didn't think she would want it alone. He hadn't meant to mention his bed, but his hurt had won in the battle between manners and truth.

How could she have gone from him to another man so quickly, and seemingly without a second thought? Not the Ally he loved.

"Your husband doesn't mind that you haven't taken his name?"

"Husband?" she asked. "I'm not married. What made you think I was married?"

Danny arched an eyebrow and glanced pointedly at her swelling stomach. She might still be wearing regular clothes, but the way her skirt was hiked up over her rounded belly was a sure indication that maternity clothing was not far away. "I've never known you to overeat, so I don't think that bulge around your middle has anything to do with the usual kind of weight gain."

"No…it doesn't," Allison said.

She paused, and Danny wondered if she would deny it.

"Yes, I am pregnant," she finally admitted.

"When are you due?" Danny asked bluntly. He might have a stake in this. After all, he was as capable of counting as anybody else. Though six months had passed since he and Ally had been together and they'd used protection, accidents did happen. From what he could see, six months was about how far along she was. After all, he came from a large family, and he'd seen a lot of pregnant women in his thirty-three years. But then, he reminded himself, Ally was a small woman and any weight gain would be magnified on her tiny frame.

"That, Sergeant Murphey, is none of your business." Allison snatched her papers off her desk and scurried out a side door, closing it firmly behind her.

"None of my business, my ass," Danny muttered as he stared at the door. He'd wanted to spend his life with this woman. He deserved to know the truth. "I will find out if you're carrying my baby if it's the last thing I do."

Then he pivoted sharply and headed after Jake Magnussen.

Even though he wasn't the least bit hungry. At least, not for food.

ALLISON SANK into her desk chair and tried to slow her racing heart. Her fingers trembled as she fumbled with a stack of notes on her desk. Finally, she gave up any pretense of trying to pretend that Danny's... reaction had surprised her.

She'd never imagined that Danny might turn up in her classroom. He'd caught her off guard.

If she'd been thinking at all, she would have thanked him for his congratulations and let him go on assuming what he had. It would have saved them both a lot of heartache. But no. She had pretty much given him more reasons to wonder.

She'd once expected to make a life with Danny. Had dreamed of growing large with his child. But when he'd issued that stupid macho ultimatum that she relinquish her job once they were married, she had walked away.

Funny, she had known that he'd had a traditional, blue-collar upbringing, and she'd certainly enjoyed some aspects of his protectiveness toward women. But she'd always assumed that she'd be able to persuade him to see her side of the issue. His refusal to bend on that one important aspect of her life, however, had definitely been a deal breaker. There was no way she'd ever spend her life dependent on a man who intended to orchestrate her life in the manner her mother had always believed was proper.

Raneea Hassim Carter had met and married Allison's father when he was an exchange student at the university in Tamahlya, Raneea's home. In spite of her traditional upbringing, they'd fallen head-over-heels in love, and Raneea's forward-thinking, college-professor father had given them his blessing. Though Raneea had attended university, she'd been content to take on a passive role in their marriage, as her grandmother had, and her mother, and her mother before her, even after she and her husband had come to the United States. She'd seldom ventured from the house and hadn't made much of an effort to learn the language of her new country.

Ally's father died when Ally was a senior in high

school in Chicago, and Raneea had been unable to accept the idea of getting a job and supporting her child. Even if she had wanted to, the language barrier would have been insurmountable. For that matter, she hadn't even been able to manage something as simple as paying the bills or balancing her checkbook. That had been a real eye-opener for Allison. Finally, her mother had gone back to Tamahlya to live with her family, and only the fact that Allison had, by that time, already entered college, kept her from being forced to leave the country herself.

Yes, she had loved her mother, but she would never allow any man to rule her life. She'd found her mother's behavior so abhorrent that she'd never really wanted to understand her or her Tamahlyan family. Courses in college had given her some appreciation of the culture she'd come from; but by then it had been too late. Her approach to life had been formed.

Allison sighed, realizing that her memories had replaced her upset. Fortunately, she did not have to teach the afternoon session. But she did have to eat lunch. Even if she wasn't hungry, she had someone else to think about.

Rapping on the jamb of her opened door startled her, and Allison looked up with a jerk.

"Sorry, I didn't mean to surprise you," Kathryn Palmore said. "When you didn't come to my office, I thought you might have forgotten our lunch date. Is there a problem with your class?"

Boy, was there! But no way would Allison drag

Kathie into it. She simply shook her head. "Just tired, I guess." She placed her hand over her expanding belly. "I didn't think carrying an extra little person around, even one this tiny, would be so exhausting." It was the truth, just not the answer to the question that Kathie had asked.

"Been there, done that," Kathie said with a laugh. "And you've been deprived of the pleasure of coffee, to boot. I swear, that was the hardest part of having all my kids. Well, the last two, anyway. The first time, they still hadn't come up with the no-caffeine rule. Or maybe I just ignored it." She made a dismiss-ive motion with her hands.

Allison pushed herself up out of the chair. "I'm with you on that one. Decaf's better than nothing, but barely. And I'm already sick of being so tired that I have to go to bed early. That is definitely for the birds."

As she took her jacket off the chair back, realized that Danny wouldn't know any good restaurants off base, so she and Kathie would be better off going to one in town, though they had originally planned to eat at the Servicemen's Club. "How about Ro-mano's? I have a craving for one of their spinach sal-ads."

The colonel laughed as Allison collected her purse from her desk drawer. "No wonder you haven't gained very much weight. Most people have cravings for fattening things like chocolate marshmallow ice cream. By the time I was six months pregnant, I was as big as the side of a barn."

"Oh, I crave chocolate," Allison confessed. "I just eat it when nobody's looking. It doesn't count then," she added, wishing fervently that were true.

"They make great chocolate cheesecake at Romano's," Kathryn said, wagging her eyebrows suggestively as Allison followed her into the corridor.

"Let's just change the subject. Have you seen the latest Reese Witherspoon movie?"

"No. Is it good?" Kathie asked as they stepped outside into the blustery, fall air.

"It's gotten some good reviews. Want to go with?"

"Maybe. I'll have to see what Robbie has to do this weekend." Kathryn's husband, Robert, had been killed in Operation Desert Storm, and Kathie had pulled herself together and gone back into the Air Force to support her children and be an example to her daughters. Robbie, the youngest, was the only one still at home. Allison admired the way Kathie had picked up the pieces and carried on. Colonel Kathryn Palmore was certainly a role model any young woman could admire.

And Allison wanted to be a similar example to her own child. She didn't need a man to cling to. She was quite capable of taking care of herself. And her baby. Thank goodness, attitudes had changed and she would face few ramifications for being single and pregnant. Of course, she would have preferred to do it the right way. But only with the right man.

Danny Murphey's antiquated beliefs had made it clear he wasn't.

She had willed herself not to think about the man

who had fathered her child—not an easy task since that moment Danny had strode into her classroom this morning. Until then, he had simply been the sperm donor. She had told herself that he did not figure in her and her baby's lives at all. Yet somewhere in the deepest recesses of her heart, she wished he did.

THE AROMAS coming from the kitchen were tempting. Danny's mouth watered as he waited in the chow line. His mood ranged from irate to curious to confused, and he welcomed to opportunity to puzzle it all out. One minute he wanted to know who had fathered Ally's child so soon after that wonderful, awful night they'd had. The next minute, he was furious.

And Danny wasn't the least bit certain whether he was angry that Ally had had the audacity to find another man so soon after she'd been with him, or that she hadn't deemed him good enough to father her child.

Then again, he wasn't so certain that he wasn't the father. The timing was about right, according to his calculations. She could have visited a sperm bank. However, Danny didn't think so. Ambitious and independent or not, she wouldn't want to go that route just to have a child.

Danny couldn't imagine her casually drifting from one man to another. And he knew the importance she'd always placed on marriage and family. To the right man.

It just hadn't been him.

They had used protection the last night they had been together, but that condom had been in his wallet for a long time....

He drew in a deep, exasperated breath. Sisters or no, he'd never really understood women, particularly educated, ambitious ones. Why in the hell had he had to fall in love with this one?

"Hey, Murph. You in there?"

Danny blinked himself out of his thoughts as Jake Magnussen waved his hand in front of his face. "Huh? What did you say?"

"You're holding up the line," a chief master sergeant, standing a couple of people back, growled.

Danny snapped to. He was standing at the silverware bin and the line in front of him had moved all the way to the dessert section.

"Sorry," he muttered, then grabbed the necessary utensils and quickly moved on, not bothering to look at what he was selecting.

"What's with you, man?" Jake challenged. "You were so fired up about taking this class and being shipped out to where the real action is, and now you're all moody about it. You change your mind?"

"No, I have not changed my mind," Danny snapped as he picked up a cup and filled it with high-test, full-caffeine coffee. They'd loaded on a C-130 transport at Hurlburt at zero-dark-thirty this morning so he could accept this last-minute opening, and he needed the jump start. Maybe if his mind was clear, he'd be able to wrap his brain around this whole Allison thing.

Maybe.

Yeah, sure.

"Well, what's got you breathing fire, then?" Magnussen was nothing if not persistent.

Danny had a good mind to tell Jake to shove it where the sun don't shine as he followed him to a vacant table. But he didn't. "I didn't get enough sleep last night," he finally said, taking a seat. Hell, he knew that was a lame excuse.

Jake started to say something, then wisely shut his mouth. Danny shrugged, sat down and started to eat. He didn't speak until he was through. Only then did he realize that he didn't even know what he'd eaten.

He had been thinking—a dangerous thing, some people might say—and he'd made up his mind. He no more believed that Allison Carter would casually have somebody's baby than he believed in the man in the moon—unless you counted Neil Armstrong.

He picked up his tray and headed for the door, not even waiting for Jake. He had to get a game plan in place, and he didn't need Jake sticking his pointed, Norwegian nose into it.

Ally was the woman he'd always dreamed of, the woman he loved. If it was the last thing he did, he was going to make Allison "I want to be independent" Carter agree to let him be the father to her baby. His baby, he was almost positive.

And he was going to marry her. Even if he had to kidnap her and carry her to the nearest justice of the peace.

Chapter Two

At least Captain Haddad was teaching the afternoon session, Allison thought with relief as she rested her chin wearily on the palm of her hand, elbow propped on her cluttered desk. She wouldn't have to face Danny again today. His accusing glares during the morning session had been bad enough, and the scene right before lunch had thoroughly unnerved her.

She'd had some time to think this afternoon, though she should have been preparing for tomorrow morning's session. She had been unfair to Danny, she realized as she began to gather her things together to take home. She hadn't really planned to…steal his "donation" that night—they had used protection—but when she'd discovered she was pregnant it had been the answer to many prayers.

She had wanted to be a mother for so long. When she and Danny were together, she'd wanted a baby, but the stupid man had ruined it all with his pig-headed, old-fashioned attitude. She'd erroneously assumed that men working side by side with women in uniform would have transcended that approach. However, as far as Danny was concerned, there could be no compromise.

At the time Ally had been nearing thirty. Since her chances of finding the right man would diminish as she got older—if published statistics were accurate—she'd reluctantly said goodbye, in the hope of finding someone else to make a life and have a child with, but on *her* terms. Later, with no man in the picture, she had even considered artificial insemination to conceive the child she wanted.

As it happened, she didn't have to.

To kill her last evening in town after attending a conference at Hurlburt Field, Florida, where Danny was stationed, she'd accepted a ticket to a Charity Bachelor Auction given to her by a sweet elderly lady in a red hat and a purple dress, who'd said that her niece couldn't use it. Among the bachelors for sale was Danny Murphey.

After Ally had realized that she'd become pregnant from that one night's reunion, she'd wondered if the lady in the red hat had been her fairy godmother making her fondest wish come true. Of course, she knew that those kinds of things only happened in fiction, not real life. But it had seemed like fate.

Karma.

Destiny.

Still, she had been so elated that that night had produced a miracle that she hadn't really considered how her situation might affect Danny.

And it had never occurred to her that he would find out.

Or that he might actually care.

Now he has found out, and he apparently does care, Allison thought as she shoved her notes for tomorrow's class into her already overstuffed briefcase. But was it a real desire to know his child that motivated him, or simply stupid macho pride. She jammed her arms through the sleeves of her coat and looped the belt loosely around her waist.

Danny was here, and had figured out she was pregnant. Now she had to figure out what to do.

DANNY HATED resorting to subterfuge, but he had already scouted out Allison's car in the staff parking lot. She still drove the same one she'd had at Hurlburt Field, so finding it hadn't been hard.

Ally wouldn't recognize the rental he'd picked up at noon. He sat in the driver's seat, motor idling, as the late-September sun began to sink behind the Headquarters Building. As much of a workaholic as Allison had been in the good old days, he couldn't imagine her staying into the night to work with a baby on board.

A recorded bugle call announced "Retreat" and Danny stepped out of his car and stood at attention as the flag in front of HQ was taken down for the day. He couldn't actually see the ceremony, but he knew what that distinctive melody meant, and he knew what he had to do.

If Ally picked this moment to come out, she was

supposed to stop, as well. Maybe she wouldn't notice him, just see him as one of many nameless, faceless airmen coming to attention as the flag came down. She didn't appear. When the last strains of "Retreat" faded, Danny relaxed and climbed back into the car to wait.

Within minutes Allison emerged from the building and headed for her car. *Yessss,* Danny cheered inwardly. *Right on time.* Ally hadn't left early, but she hadn't lingered, either.

Danny watched as she'd stowed her bags in the back seat, settled herself into the car, turned on the engine and pulled out of her slot. Once she'd steered out to the main road, he pulled out behind her.

ALLY DRUMMED HER FINGERS impatiently against the steering wheel as she idled at the red light on the congested road leading out of the base. She just wanted to go home, where she could relax and unwind. Maybe five in the afternoon didn't seem late to anybody else, but to Allison Carter it might as well have been midnight. Every muscle in her body ached with a kind of fatigue she'd never experienced. This wasn't the normal pregnancy weariness she'd been having so far. This feeling was something entirely different.

It was because of Danny. Of that she was certain.

Her fatigue was easily explained. It was from the tension of wondering what Technical Sergeant Daniel Xavier Murphey was going to do next.

So far so good, though, she thought with relief.

She'd made it through the day without any more scenes from Danny, so maybe that was the extent of the problems he would cause. Maybe Danny had just needed to let off some steam, and he'd let her be from now on.

Maybe she'd convinced him that the baby she was carrying was not his, even if it was and even if she longed with every fiber of her being to acknowledge him as the father. Not only that, but she wanted so much to be gathered into his arms and to enjoy that safe and protected feeling that only Danny could give her.

Of course, she'd ruined any chance of that happening by her refusal to satisfactorily respond to his probing this morning.

An impatient driver leaning on his car horn brought her to attention. The light had turned green while she'd been woolgathering. She quickly eased out onto the main road, the better to avoid the wrath of an entire crew of tired workers angry at her for keeping them from their homes and their dinners.

She had leftover homemade soup in the fridge. Nothing would make her happier than to kick off her shoes, slip into her most comfortable old sweats, heat up the soup in the microwave and just sit. She'd have the rest of the evening to regenerate and to rehearse what she would say if Danny confronted her again.

Of course, she'd hoped she wouldn't have to give any speech, but it was always better to be prepared. If she'd anticipated seeing him, she probably should have been prepared to face Danny, instead of assuming that he was out of her life for good. If she had, their encounter might have gone better than it had this morning.

After all, the military, as spread out as it was, had always been a small community, more like a small town than a giant corporation. News traveled fast, and even if Danny hadn't appeared in her classroom this morning, one of the other members of Silver Team based at Hurlburt Field in Florida could easily have gone there and reported back to him.

She really should have been prepared, she chided herself.

Ally drew up in front of her small, ranch-style house and paused long enough to retrieve the mail from the box at the side of the road and scoop up the newspaper, clothed in a bright orange plastic bag. That portended rain. What else did she need to polish off her crummy day? She jabbed the remote to open the garage door.

A car cruised by as she steered hers into the garage. It wasn't a car she'd noticed in the neighborhood before, and its leisurely pace indicated that the driver was probably looking for a house number. The vehicle hadn't stopped at her house, so as far as Ally was concerned, the problem was somebody else's.

The garage door closed behind her and Ally sighed in relief. She was home.

She was safe.

She didn't have to think about Danny Murphey again until 0730.

"WHEW. THAT WAS CLOSE," Danny told himself as he passed Ally's house. He made a U-turn farther down the street, then cruised back up and idled in front of a house a couple of lots down from hers. He figured he'd best reconnoiter the situation first. If there really was a man in Ally's life, he wanted to know about him. He damn sure didn't want to intrude on somebody else's domestic tranquility. If there was any.

For a woman who'd placed her career before him, Ally sure had a homey little house. Hell, it was everything any woman would want, except for, maybe, the missing picket fence. But then, he wasn't sure they even made them anymore.

The lawn was neat and tidy, and mounds of brightly colored flowers lined the sidewalk. Window boxes dripped with some ivylike stuff, and the tiny front porch had one of those clay pots with the holes in the sides. He couldn't see what she'd planted in it, but he'd bet something was there.

He watched as the lights went on, making the cozy-looking house look even warmer, more welcoming. First in what must have been a kitchen, then the living room and then in a room toward the far end of the house, which must have been her bedroom.

A quiver of envy for the man who had slept with her crept to the front of his mind, but Danny pushed it back. He was here to see if anyone else came home before he confronted Ally one more time.

As much as she had protested that the child she was carrying was not his, something in his gut told him it was. If another man did show up at her house tonight, then Danny would quietly back away and no one would be the wiser. If she was alone, then he'd take his chances.

Tonight might be the only chance he'd get.

Danny waited until the sound of his stomach grumbling seemed to drown out the radio. So far, no man had driven up, and he figured that both he and Allison still had to eat. *He* might be eating for one, but Ally was eating for two.

He could go pick up a pizza. If a man did turn up, he'd be able to tell because Ally's garage was made for one car. If there was another car in the driveway when he got back, he'd drive on by.

Besides, if the way to a man's heart was through the stomach, surely it was the way to a pregnant woman's, Danny thought as he pulled away from the curb and headed back to a strip mall he'd passed on the way. He'd noticed a pizza place there. He just hoped they were quick.

WAS THIS WHAT PEOPLE MEANT by nesting? Ally wondered as she contemplated lighting the gas logs in the living room. Maybe September was a little early for a fire, but the gray sky outside and the promise of rain made her long for the coziness a fire in the fireplace provided. She liked the notion of being cocooned and safe and warm.

With the sudden appearance of Danny Murphey in town, her comfortable world seemed threatened. She shivered with unease and hugged herself to ward off the uncomfortable feeling. Then she lit the fire. She had a gas fireplace so she could easily turn it off if the room got too hot.

She settled down on the couch, comfortable now in cozy socks and an extra-large sweatsuit, and tucked her legs beneath her. She'd eaten her soup, and she was enjoying a cup of hot chocolate, her one indulgence for today—not counting the chocolate cheesecake she'd shared with Kathie at lunch. The fire, the chocolate, the comfy clothes made her feel safe and secure.

Then somebody rang the doorbell.

Reluctantly, Ally uncurled from the couch and made her way to the door. For a moment, she regretted not having a peephole or a window near the door. It was probably just one of the local kids selling candy for fund-raising or something like that. She'd always supported their causes, and saw no reason to stop now. Plus, she'd have a sweet on hand when the urge struck.

But something made her pause before she opened the door. Some little shred of caution made her call out, "Who is it?"

"Delivery service," came from a muffled voice to the other side of the door.

Ally wrinkled her brow. She didn't remember ordering anything recently. "Are you certain you have the right house?" she called through the still-locked door. "I'm not expecting a delivery."

"Is this 924 Allegheny?"

"Yes."

"Your name Carter?"

Whoever it was knew her name. She wasn't certain whether to acknowledge that or not. "Just leave whatever it is on the step," she suggested. That was what they usually did.

"Look, lady. I gotta get a signature here. You either sign, or I take it back. Makes no difference to me. I gotta get moving, though. You ain't the only delivery I got tonight," he added, a note of irritation entering his voice.

Allison hesitated, undecided what to do. She often got deliveries this late and, on occasion, out-of-stock items that had finally arrived so long after she'd ordered them that she'd forgotten all about them. She supposed it could be one of those.

"All right." She pretended to call toward the back of the house. "It's okay, Fred. It's just a delivery-man."

She opened the door, and Danny Murphey, carrying a pizza box, stepped inside.

"Why don't you invite *Fred* to join us," he said sarcastically as he lowered the box. His tone told her he wasn't fooled by her ruse, and his cocky grin, so familiar and endearing, opened his handsome face.

"You know there's no Fred," Ally said. She couldn't decide whether to be pleased or annoyed at Danny's ingenuity. And she was flattered at the same time. All she knew was that she had eaten a light dinner and right now the pizza smelled awfully good. Her mouth watered, and her stomach clamored in agreement.

Still, she stood her ground by the door, held it

open and pointed outside. "There's the exit," she said. "Please use it."

Danny simply strode past her, placed the pizza box on the coffee table by the half-empty mug of chocolate and lifted the lid. The rich aroma of tomatoes and spices, stronger now that the box was open, filled the room.

The pizza was tempting, but she had to get Danny to leave. Again, she pointed the way. "I said, get out."

Her effort was futile. Danny ignored her and made himself comfortable on the couch. He selected a wedge of pizza and took a bite.

"It's really good," he said, his mouth full.

He chewed for a moment while Allison stood by the door and wondered what to do.

Danny patted the couch cushion beside him and took another bite. "There's plenty for both of us," he said, gesturing toward her with his half-eaten slice.

An empty spot in her stomach that she hadn't realized she hadn't filled earlier, plus the fragrant steam coming off the pizza, weakened Allison's resolve. She closed the door, careful not to turn the lock in case she needed to open the door in a hurry.

The pizza ploy had finally worn her down. Darn it. And as much as Danny's attitude annoyed her, she still loved the man. In spite of herself. In spite of everything. Of course, Ally was aware that Danny might be irritating and exasperating at times, but he was a good man. He would never hurt her. Not physically, anyway. It was what he might do to her heart that really worried her.

"Thank you for the pizza, Danny," she said, using sarcasm to disguise her gratitude as she reached into the box and selected a piece. She settled into a chair across from the sofa where Danny sat.

"I figured I could get you with black-olive-and-mushroom pizza," Danny said, looking smug.

But Ally was too hungry to argue; she let his remark ride.

Neither of them spoke as they ate. Finally, there was one piece left. "Do you want it?" Allison asked.

Danny shrugged. "Nope. I've had plenty. You're eating for two, remember?"

It was the first mention of the baby. However, the comment seemed innocuous enough. Ally shrugged. "All right, I can put it in the fridge for later. Are you going to leave now?" Maybe her question was rude, but the tension of having Danny so close was wearing on her. She had to consider the baby.

"Won't be long," Danny said with a satisfied expression. He held out his hands. "I have to wash up."

"Oh. Sure," Ally said, pointing toward the back of the house. "Second door on the left."

Wondering why she hadn't just sent him to the kitchen, Ally watched Danny go. She couldn't help noting his well-shaped butt as he went, and she mentally chastised herself.

Danny wasn't gone long. "You sure you're not gonna eat that piece?" he said as he sat back down.

"You can have it if you want it," Ally replied,

loath to admit that she really could have downed that last piece.

"And I said you were eating for two and you need it," Danny reminded her. "Take it."

As she did, Danny reached for her wrist and held her fast by the hand.

"Wh-what do you want?" Ally stammered as she let go of the slice and tried to free her trapped hand.

Danny held on and looked at her with angry green eyes. "Come off it, Allison. You know exactly what I want. And if you don't, let me spell it out for you. I know you well enough to be damned sure that you wouldn't have tumbled into bed with me if there had been anyone else in your life. I also know that you don't leap casually from man to man and bed to bed.

"I did a little recon while I was in your bathroom," he continued. Danny released her hand, and Ally rubbed it reflexively. "I saw no evidence of a man having been there. Not on even a semipermanent basis," he said with satisfaction. "And unless you've had a personality transplant since we went our separate ways, you haven't been sleeping around. I figure you didn't hook up with anyone soon enough after we were together to already be having his baby."

"Get to the point, Danny," Allison managed to say, though she was pretty sure she knew what he was about to say. How she found her voice or the strength to get up off the couch, she didn't know.

"That baby is mine," he said with as much certainty as he would his own name. "I figure we have a few things to settle."

Allison paled visibly, her olive skin taking on a greenish cast, and Danny figured he'd hit the truth right on the mark.

He should have felt good about that, but it wasn't the triumph it might have been. After all, the woman had lied to him, even though it had been by omission. And if he hadn't just happened to walk into her classroom this morning, she might have kept right on doing so.

Ally swallowed, or maybe she gulped, then she swallowed again. "What do we have to settle?"

Ally wasn't that dense, so obviously she was still trying to stonewall him. "Give it up, Ally. That's my baby you're carrying." He'd wanted Ally from almost the moment they'd met, and now he wanted the child. And it would require more than an on-the-knee proposal to get that to happen. Hell, he'd been there, done that, and the wedding hadn't happened.

Ally grew paler yet, if that was possible. "No," she protested. "She's mine."

"She? You mean you already know what you're having and you hadn't even bothered to tell me I am going to be a father?" Danny said, disgusted.

"I'm not sure what sex the baby is, but I thought it would be easier to think of it as a her."

She stopped. Why was she explaining to him? "It takes more than being a sperm donor to be a father," Allison countered.

She might not have realized it, but that pretty much cinched things for Danny. She had all but admitted the baby was his.

"So, is that what you had in mind the night you paid for my services?" He didn't know whether to be insulted or flattered.

Appearing none too steady on her feet, Allison sank slowly back to the couch. "I didn't pay for... services," she said weakly.

Danny arched an eyebrow. "Oh, yeah. You might not have paid me, but you damn sure paid somebody. Did you get your money's worth from that bachelor auction?"

Allison gasped and reacted as though he'd slapped her in the face, but the color that had drained from her cheeks had begun to return. "That auction was for charity," she protested.

"Oh, so you're telling me that your showing up to bid on me was a convenient accident. There's no way you can convince me that you just happened to be hundreds of miles away from here and in Florida the very Friday I was drafted into that..." He groped for the right word. "That...blasted auction." To even finish the thought was too absurd.

"'Coincidence'? Is that the word you're looking for, Danny?" His indecisiveness had apparently allowed Ally to find her voice. She went on. "Yes, it was a pure coincidence. I was in Florida, at Hurlburt Field, for a conference. I just happened to run into an elderly lady as I was on the way into the dining room for dinner. She said that her niece was supposed to have come with her and couldn't come. She offered me her extra ticket.

"It seemed like fun," she added, shrugging. "I was

facing a long night alone in the hotel before I could get my flight out in the morning, so I took the ticket. I didn't know you'd be there. If I had, I would never have…" She let her voice trail off.

"I just wanted a way to kill an evening. I didn't have anything to read, and I'd gotten tired of staying inside and watching television…to keep from running into you," she added in a voice so low that Danny almost didn't hear it.

That admission proved to him that Allison wasn't nearly as over him as she claimed to be. "So you decided it was time to have a baby, and you knew that I'd be a willing sperm donor. Well, I have a news flash for you, Allison. I didn't donate anything to you. What you took, you took under false pretenses. My half of the DNA of that baby—our baby—was stolen! I wonder what a judge would have to say about that!"

"You wouldn't."

"I wouldn't what?"

"You wouldn't take this to court," Ally said weakly. How had it come to this? What had seemed like such a simple solution to her need to be a mother had suddenly become very complicated. There was no way she was going to give Danny any more ammunition to use against her. "Besides, we used protection."

"Which you could easily have sabotaged!" Danny countered.

Ally rolled her eyes. She started to say something, but bit back her retort. She didn't want to argue. "Go away, Danny. Leave me alone," she said tiredly.

She had to get herself together. Maybe she had been wrong in sleeping with Danny when they were no longer together, but she'd sensed that they'd still had a connection even after two long years apart. She'd hoped that they might be able to reconnect, create a future for themselves this time.

Then he'd ruined it all, assuming that by sleeping with him, she had suggested that she would change her mind about giving up her career and all that she held important. He'd told her that he wanted to take care of her, as if she were a child, incapable of thinking and doing for herself. The pure arrogance of the man!

Until that moment, Ally'd had such high hopes that they might still have a future. Then she'd heard him utter those words. He didn't know that she'd heard his confident declaration that night while she was asleep—or so he'd thought. In the cold light of the morning after, she'd known that they weren't going to make it as a couple.

Until Danny changed his attitudes, they couldn't be together.

"Please, Danny. Leave us alone. All this anger and stress aren't good for…the baby," she murmured. She hated to play the baby card, but it was the only thing she had left. And she didn't have the energy to deal with anything else tonight.

Maybe not ever.

"Okay, Allison. You win for now, but this is in no

way over. Not by a long shot." Danny pushed himself to his feet and headed for the door, but then he turned back and looked at her over his shoulder. "I will be back to finish this."

That was what Ally was afraid of, but she wasn't going to say it. She didn't need to provide Danny Murphey with any clues to what she was thinking, anything that he might use against her later on.

She watched, vainly trying to keep her lips from trembling. She managed to keep from breaking into tears until he'd gone, then she hurried to the door and locked it.

As she walked away, thinking she should have been relieved that Danny was gone, a sudden barrage of pounding against the door almost gave her a heart attack, and she clutched at her throat as she tried to get her heartbeat to return to normal.

"Come on, Ally. Open up."

"No," she shouted through the door. "I can't deal with anything else today."

"I forgot something," Danny called.

Ally closed her eyes and drew in a deep, weary breath. If she didn't let him in, he'd make enough noise to disturb the neighbors. They'd been okay with her unwed status, but she wasn't sure her standing in the neighborhood would be enhanced by Danny's making a scene.

She glanced around the room for what he might have left. "I don't see anything, Danny. What is it?"

"Let me in."

She just couldn't continue to let Danny bother the

neighbors, so she reluctantly opened the door. He seemed to fill the doorway with his handsome presence, and Allison instinctively stepped back. "All right, get it and get out. What did you forget, anyway?"

"This—" he said, grabbing her by the shoulders and hauling her to him.

Chapter Three

Of course he shouldn't have done it, but the moment he stepped out the door, he knew he wouldn't be able to sleep tonight until he'd tasted her lips again. By God, he was going to kiss her. Considering he was about to be shipped out to the Middle East soon, this might be his last chance.

He had looked down into Ally's dark gray eyes and saw fear. Her heart had beat frantically against him as he pressed her to his chest. She'd balled her fists, but she hadn't struggled. He hated that he'd made her afraid, and he had to try to assure her that he had no evil intent. But, how the hell did he do that? If he tried to explain, she'd only argue with him. Ally had always been so much better with words than he was.

So Danny had done the one thing he'd wanted to do all along. He drew her closer, tipped her face up to his and kissed her. His intent had been simply to drop a kiss on her lips and leave, but he quickly discovered that one kiss was not enough.

Trying not to be too demanding, he went back for more. Her mouth, which at first had been so unyielding, softened beneath his lips. She returned the kiss, tentatively at first, then with more confidence. Her velvety lips parted to let him in, and he felt more than heard her moan of pleasure.

When she wrapped her arms around him and began to play with the hair at his nape, he knew he'd won, hollow victory that it was.

He also knew that if he kept at this, he'd want to take her to bed. As much as he ached for her, he had to stop this now. She was no longer his, and he had no right to her. Even if he planned to do everything he could to make her his again.

In the meantime, they had to think rationally. And he was well aware that when they were in bed together, they never did much thinking.

He jerked away from her, and was rewarded by the look of confusion in Ally's eyes. "I just wanted to feel you in my arms again, Ally. I didn't mean to force myself on you. I'll go, but remember this. We're not done."

He yanked open the door and strode down the tidy little walk to his car. Danny knew he'd be lost if he looked back, so he kept his gaze trained forward. He climbed into the car, started the engine and drove away.

But not without regrets.

Lots of regrets.

ALLY STOOD INSIDE the door, her hand to her kiss-swollen lips, and wondered what had just happened.

That Danny had kissed her like that wasn't a surprise, not really. He'd always been a take-charge man, and he was used to getting what he wanted.

Except for her.

He was a wonderful kisser, and though she'd tried, Ally hadn't been able to forget the way she'd always felt in his arms.

Still, the passion of her response had shocked her. They had been apart so long. Why wasn't she over him? She had thought that she'd been so rational with her plan to raise the child alone. She had thought that she had it all figured out.

However, almost the minute she was alone with Danny, she'd fallen into his arms. She hadn't wanted to show Danny how she still felt about him, but now she was pretty sure he did.

She might have been able to lie to him from across the room, she thought as she leaned against the door, but the moment he'd touched her, her body had given her away. Danny had always been able to read her, and she'd all but given him the encyclopedia.

It was a pretty darn big, wonderful kiss, and she'd enjoyed every moment of it. Until Danny had pushed her away.

Ally turned the lock on the front door and it snicked shut, then she wandered toward her bedroom, vaguely remembering to put out the lights as she went. She had too much to process, too much to work through, to consider details like shutting down the house for the night. Fortunately, her body worked on automatic and took care of the mundane tasks.

As much as she'd claimed to be an independent woman, the prospect of raising this child alone—Danny's child, she reminded herself—terrified her. She might have claimed that she wanted to be thoroughly modern and thoroughly independent, but she didn't. She wanted a home, a husband, a family and a career. And most of all, she wanted Danny to be part of her—no, their—child's life.

Now she just had to figure out how to make it happen.

AS HE DROVE through the dark and unfamiliar streets, Danny Murphey had time to think. Time to work things out in his head—something that he usually didn't do. He was, after all, a man of action, of impulse, and it was obvious that he would have to proceed with cool, calm deliberation.

He had to win Ally back. Had to convince her that he was willing to give a little if she would. If she would, he could take a lot. He wasn't used to compromising, but he could if it meant that he and Ally would be together in the end.

Danny was pretty sure that just telling Ally that he might compromise wouldn't do the trick. He'd have to show her.

Lucky for him, he had this time on temporary duty here to make his case.

A SHINY, RED APPLE SAT in a prominent position on her desk when she came into the classroom, and Ally didn't need an FBI investigation to know who had left it there. Danny Murphey was already in his seat, head bent over his textbook, and he was acting just like a little boy who had been caught with his hand in the cookie jar.

He looked up and smiled at her with the same angelic expression that had first attracted her to him over two years ago, and Ally couldn't help smiling back.

Maybe they would be able to make it through the day without incident. If Danny behaved and didn't start her heart racing. As if reading her mind, Danny winked at her.

"Good morning, Miss Carter," he said in a childish singsong as a few more members of the class filed in.

Though she tried not to, Ally laughed, and it felt good. More surprising, she discovered that the little gesture had already brightened her day.

Allison cleared her throat, wiped her hands on the skirt of her business-appropriate suit and called the class to order. "Today's lesson will focus on local traditions in some of the areas you will be serving," she told them. "Although the women are no longer required to wear the tentlike burkhas you probably remember seeing on the television news, they are required by law to maintain a strict code of modesty, and many older women do still feel more comfortable being covered up.

"I guess old habits are hard to break," she said with a smile, thinking about the handsome, redhaired man leaning back in his chair in the third row, apparently trying to be unobtrusive.

"Not only that," she continued, "in many countries a woman is not permitted to go out alone or
speak to a man who is not a member of her family
if she is not properly chaperoned. Even something
as innocent as a handshake with someone of the opposite sex is not permitted."

She glanced around the classroom and waited for
the information to sink in. Ally suspected that most
of her students already knew this, but the next bit of
information she would deliver would probably be
new. "Moreover, it would be considered in our best
interest to observe their customs, not try to inflict
ours on them."

An eager female lieutenant, blond and blue-
eyed—and a service academy graduate, Ally knew
from her paperwork—raised her hand. "Excuse me,
Ms. Carter. Does that mean we should avoid speaking to the natives?"

"They're not 'natives,' Lieutenant. You may call
them locals or indigenous people, but let's give them
the same respect you would expect.

"In answer to your question, Lieutenant, yes. Especially refrain from man-woman exchanges. In fact,
try to avoid contact with the locals unless absolutely
necessary," Ally added. "Let me also mention—and
you need to remember this—that you must take care
not to appear in public without a male escort."

The lieutenant raised her hand again and, without
waiting to be called on, blurted, "But we're not members of their society, and I'm not about to start kow-
towing to men and walking three steps behind." She

looked as though she wanted to say more, but Ally stopped her by holding up her hand.

"Relations with some of these countries are quite strained, Lieutenant Abernathy. We must be certain not to do anything that might jeopardize our mission there. Have you heard the expression 'When in Rome, do as the Romans do'?"

Looking doubtful, her lips pursed, the lieutenant nodded.

"Then do it," Danny Murphey interjected, staring pointedly at the woman.

Lieutenant Abernathy rolled her eyes. "Obviously, you didn't spend four years at the Air Force Academy, Sergeant," the woman retorted. "I didn't work like a dog trying to prove I was as good as any man there, to be sent to Tamahlyastan on my first assignment and have to go around wearing a tent and trotting behind a man like a trained puppy."

"I didn't say you had to *wear* a burkha," Allison interjected, knowing that Danny was sure to comment on that. He had never minced words when dealing with "overeducated" academy grads.

Danny held up his hands in a gesture of surrender. "Nobody said you had to act like a…dumb blonde, Lieutenant," he said. "Just follow the rules. You can do that, can't you? Isn't that what you had to do at the Academy?" He appeared ready to say something else, but Ally shot him a quelling glance, and Danny had the good sense to quit while he was ahead.

"You can still use your brains and your education," Ally explained, hoping to ease the situation. "You just have to respect the local customs when you are out in public. You're there to act as ambassadors as well as to work. When you're at your post, doing your job, you're under no obligation to observe custom. It's only when you're outside. Don't act like the Ugly Americans so many people in those societies perceive us to be."

Clearly, the lieutenant didn't want to leave it at that. "Well, I think it's ridiculous."

"Lieutenant Abernathy," Danny said, and Ally held her breath, hoping that he wouldn't say something stupid. "Do you stand at attention when the flag is raised?"

"Yes."

"When you're in civvies, do you put your hand over your heart and stand when they play the national anthem at ball games?"

"Yes."

"Do you like it when a man holds the door open for you even when you are perfectly capable of doing it yourself?"

"Yes. What's your point, Sergeant?" the lieutenant finally asked, obviously tiring of the exercise.

Ally, too, was curious about Danny's point.

"All those—" he groped for the right word "—gestures are not required by law. They're traditions—customs, if you want—not laws. We don't have monitors making sure you do them, but you do them anyway."

"Yes," the lieutenant answered slowly, her brows knitted in puzzlement.

"Well, those are all customs that you observe that someone from another country might think are stupid. Am I right?"

Score one for Danny Murphey, Ally thought with approval. Maybe he had matured a little since they'd been together several years ago.

"I get your point," the lieutenant said begrudgingly. She glanced up at Ally. "I'm sorry, Ms. Carter. Go on with your presentation."

DANNY REMAINED SEATED until the rest of the class had left for lunch. Today, Ally hadn't ducked out the rear door. That fact was enough to give him hope. He leaned back in his chair and watched as she deliberately gathered up her materials and stacked them neatly in a pile. She retrieved the disk for her PowerPoint presentation, then turned to him.

"Are you free for lunch, Sergeant?" she asked, surprising the hell out of him. He'd thought he'd have to make the first move.

"Thought you'd never ask, Teach," he replied, sliding out of his seat. "Your place or mine?" He grinned, knowing she wouldn't go for that one.

Ally's mouth twitched as she tried to suppress a smile. "The club will be fine," she said primly as she buttoned the jacket of the suit over her stomach. The buttons strained across her growing belly. "I'll pay."

Danny wouldn't protest. It was an old argument between the two of them, and one he'd never once won. The best he'd been able to negotiate was Dutch treat.

Danny held the classroom door open and waited for Ally to step through. Even with her belly swelling with his child, she moved with fluid grace. Danny made no effort to disguise his appreciation of the view. For a small woman she had terrific legs, even if she had apparently given up wearing high, high heels in deference to her pregnancy.

"Still a leg man, I see," Ally said as she brushed by him.

"Can't get anything past you, can I."

Ally chuckled. "Not when it's that blatant. You could make an effort to be more discreet."

"Oh, I can be when I need to," Danny said, remembering his stealth campaign of the previous evening. He shrugged, then touched the small of Ally's back and urged her forward. She seemed a little softer than he remembered, but then, he supposed that was to be expected. "Considering you're pretty well checked out on all my moves, I figured I didn't need to hide anything. You know what I want."

"That I do, Danny," she said, a lighthearted expression on her face. "That I do. However, you could have learned some new moves since…"

She didn't continue, but Danny understood exactly what she meant. *Since I left you.* But, then she'd probably turn the argument around and say he'd left her by not being willing to see things her way.

Danny shook himself out of those morose thoughts. He'd succeeded in getting her to go to lunch with him—well, actually, she'd beaten him to the punch, and that was even better. Score one for his team.

He didn't try to hide his satisfied smile.

"I saw it, Danny. You never could hide anything from me," Ally said. "You don't exactly have a poker face."

"Only where you're concerned," Danny protested, but Ally shushed him with a gentle touch of a finger to his lips.

"Seriously, though. I appreciated the way you handled the lieutenant this morning. I was afraid she was going to be a real problem child."

"I guess maybe this old dog has learned a few new tricks since we were…together." Danny grinned. "I may not have been born with a generous helping of tact, but I'm not stupid. I can be taught." He shrugged as he held open the door that led outside.

The lesson had been difficult and hard to take, but when he'd been angry at the world after Ally had taken off the first time, he'd entered into a real shouting match with the major and had barely escaped serious trouble. Fortunately, Lieutenant Marx, new to the squadron at the time, had taken him aside and given him a few pointers, a lesson he hadn't been particularly interested in then, but one that had eventually sunk in.

"Good to know," Ally replied. She stood at the edge of the parking lot and surveyed the scattering of cars still in the lot. "Do you want to walk to the club or drive? It isn't far."

The late-September sky was a clear Air-Force-blue; there wasn't a cloud or even a hint of humidity. A breeze played with a loose strand of Ally's hair and carried with it a hint of fall. It was a perfect day for a walk.

"Is it okay?" he asked. "With you being…?"

"Pregnant? It isn't a dirty word, Danny. It's a natural process. It happens to women all over the world every day." She turned and began walking toward the club, a few blocks away.

"I know," he said defensively. "But I've never been the…"

Chapter Four

"Father?"

Danny stopped. She'd said the word so easily, voicing the concept as though it was nothing. To him it was still something he had a hard time wrapping his brain around, even if Ally had finally confirmed it.

"Yeah," he said huskily. "The father."

"Come on. Both of us are hungry." Ally tugged on his arm impatiently. "The exercise is good for us."

"Okay," Danny said. "Do you mean us, like you and me? Or you and the baby?" He paused, then added, "But I'm paying for my own."

"Works for me," Ally said, tossing him a dazzling smile. "And in answer to your question—both of the above."

Danny laughed and raised an eyebrow. "What, no protest? After all, you invited me. I should expect you to pay." In the old days, Ally would have argued until any man opposing her had no choice but to give in.

She had always had to show that she could do things on her own. Maybe she was mellowing, too.

Ally chuckled, looped her arm through his, and pulled him along. "Come on. This isn't a date. It's just two friends enjoying a meal together. Besides, it's all-you-can-eat Italian day. I have a craving for eggplant parmigiana."

"It figures." Ally had always had a fondness for pasta and any of the stuff that went with it.

Danny grinned and let her lead him along. He liked hearing Ally laugh, and the lightness of her mood encouraged him. She really seemed to be trying, but he knew better than to assume that coming out ahead in one skirmish meant he'd won the war.

ALLY WATCHED Danny dispatch his spaghetti and meatballs with his usual gusto. If she ate the way he did, she'd gain double the normal pregnancy weight. She realized she would gain more weight eventually, but she didn't want to go overboard.

Something fluttered in her stomach and she gently pressed her hand against it and smiled to herself. Even eating in her usual, sensible fashion, she was going to be big soon enough.

"What's the smile for?" Danny asked between bites.

Odd, Ally hadn't thought he could possibly have seen that little quirk of her lips, as busy as he was scarfing down his pasta. "I was just comparing your eating habits with mine," she said, not elaborating.

Danny shrugged. "Yeah. What else is new? You

never did eat enough to keep a canary alive." He glanced across the table to her nearly empty plate and arched one tawny eyebrow. "Until now."

Ally had to smile. "That's what I was thinking about." She chuckled. "I'm afraid I'm going to be huge pretty soon, no matter what I do."

"People say pregnant women are beautiful," Danny answered simply. "And you are," he added huskily.

If Ally hadn't been in love with him for years, she would have fallen for him now.

"Can I ask you something?" he said abruptly, putting his fork down and giving her his full attention.

Ally tucked a stray lock of hair behind her ear. "Depends on what it is," she replied slowly. The subject of marriage was out. "I can't guarantee I'll give you the answer you want."

Danny drew in a deep breath, almost as if he were gathering his nerve. He paused, started to speak, then closed his mouth again and thought for a moment. "I'm trying to figure out how to phrase this in just the right way."

"No, I won't marry you," Ally said. "If that's what you were thinking about asking."

"No, it wasn't," Danny said. "I'm not going to ask that until I'm reasonably certain I'll get the answer I want."

"I'm not sure you'll ever get it, Danny." Why did he have to go and ruin a perfectly pleasant lunch by bringing that up?

Danny picked the napkin up off his lap and waved

it in the air. "I give up. Let's declare a truce for the time being and just work on getting to understand where each of us is coming from."

"Okay," Ally agreed reluctantly. "You know my opinion about being a stay-at-home wife."

"Yes, Ally," Danny said, shaking his napkin out and placing it back in his lap. "I read you loud and clear. That's not what I was going to ask." He paused again. "Look, you and I come from very different family situations. Your dad was a well-educated, cultural anthropologist. Mine worked in a shoe factory and held down a second job on the weekends just to keep food on the table."

"Yes, Danny, I'm well aware of that. And you had eight kids in your family, and I was an only child. I understand." Ally sighed, wondering if their "discussion" was going to give her indigestion. "What was your question?"

Danny leaned back in his chair. "I can completely relate to your need to work and support yourself as a single woman," he said simply. "That you were smart and educated were things that attracted me to you."

"Just my brains and education?" Ally couldn't help asking as she shot him a teasing smile.

Danny grinned, displaying that familiar mischievous, little-boy expression. "That and your cute, heart-shaped behind," he added, winking.

Ally wasn't quite sure how to take that. "Just when did you ever see my behind before we were properly introduced?"

"We were at a party in Fort Walton Beach. You

were somebody else's date then, and you were wearing a red, one-piece bathing suit. The first time I saw you, you were bent over a drink cooler or something, and I got a great view of your backside, red swimsuit and all." He grinned.

"Oh," Ally said. *Best leave that topic alone for now,* she thought. It would be a long time before she would consider putting her growing body into any swimsuit, much less a bright red one. A pup tent sounded good at the moment. "You said you wanted to ask me something," she prodded. They did have to get back after lunch.

"Like I said," Danny continued, "I understand about a single woman working, but I never really understood why you were so damn dead set against giving it up once you didn't *have to work.* As I recall, you said your mother never worked."

Even now that memory poked at a sore spot in Ally's heart that hadn't healed. "No, she didn't. She never wrote a check, or paid a bill, or even learned to drive a car."

"You said your mother met your father when she was a student at the university in Tamahlya? Surely she could have handled more responsibility."

"My mother's father was quite progressive regarding equality for women, but her mother had been raised in a more traditional way," Ally explained. "My mother enjoyed learning, but she hadn't really considered ever using her education once she became a mother. Perhaps if they'd stayed in Tamahlya, she might have taught, but when they came to the

United States after Daddy accepted the teaching position in Chicago, she never seemed to fit in.

"I don't know whether she didn't want to make the effort or whether the move was too overwhelming for her." Ally sighed. "She found English difficult to master, and she was self-conscious about her broken English and her inability to communicate well. Rather than go out and try, she preferred to stay at home as her mother had."

"And since she couldn't speak the language, she couldn't pass the driver's test, or write a check, or pay a bill," Danny concluded as he reached for his water glass. "But I still don't see why that made you so determined not to let a man take care of you. Obviously, you know how to do all that."

"It's because of what happened after Daddy died," Ally said, steeling herself for the hurt that would come with the telling.

"Didn't he leave her provided for?"

"Sure. He had all sorts of savings plans, insurance and all that."

"So…?"

Danny still looked as though he was going to have a hard time understanding. Even after all these years, Ally had difficulty comprehending what had come next, what had influenced her determination to be her own woman.

Ally glanced up and was startled at what she saw. "Oh, no!" she exclaimed. The club dining room was virtually empty. She glanced at her watch. "We're going to have to continue this later. We're already late." She blotted her lips with her napkin and signaled for their waiter.

Danny checked his watch and made a face. "I can double-time it and I probably won't be late. Or I can stay and walk you back. After all, I could score an excuse from the teacher, couldn't I?"

Ally made a face. "I don't have a class this afternoon. It won't matter if I get back to my office a few minutes late. You need to get back. Go on," she said, shooing him off with her hands. "I'll take care of this."

She could read the reluctance in Danny's eyes, but he pushed himself up out of the chair.

"Okay," he said. "You pick up the check this time," he said. "But the next one's on me."

"All right," Ally said, digging in her purse.

"Don't forget," Danny said, looking back over his shoulder. "You still have to tell me the rest of the story. I want to understand. And," he added as he strode toward the exit, "I'm pretty sure you just agreed on another date with me."

Ally just shook her head and smiled as she watched Danny hurry out of the dining room.

That was a big change from the Danny she used to know, she couldn't help thinking as she picked up her check and hurried to the register. Back in the old days, he would never have let her pay for him, much less been willing to listen to her reasons.

Maybe there was hope for them yet.

His arms laden with packages and sacks, Danny stood outside Ally's front door and hoped that she wouldn't go ballistic when she got a look at what he'd done. After grabbing a fast-food supper, he'd embarked on a major shopping spree at a local baby store, all but maxing out one of his credit cards. He figured he was six months behind on getting ready for the baby, so he had some catching up to do.

Besides, Ally had promised to tell him the rest of her story. He really wanted to understand. He wasn't certain he could yield to her wishes, but he guessed he owed it to her to listen.

Ally had to be home, because lights were on, and he could hear the radio, or maybe the TV, coming from inside. He prepared himself for an argument, and rang the bell. Maybe he should have phoned first.

"Who is it?" she called from inside.

At least she was careful when the doorbell rang after dark, Danny applauded silently.

"It's me. Danny," he said, hoping his name wouldn't send her running.

"Go away, Danny. It's late, and I'm tired."

Danny could tell by the weariness in her voice that she meant it, so he counted silently to three and delivered the coup de grâce. "I brought some stuff…for the baby," he said through the closed door. "Just let me leave it…and then I'll go." Oh, he wanted to stay, but there was nothing to gain by pushing his luck. He had time.

The door opened a crack, and Ally peered warily through the securely hooked burglar chain. Her eyes widened with surprise when she saw the quantity of stuff he'd purchased in little more than an hour since class had been dismissed.

"What have you done?" she muttered as she fumbled with the chain.

"I figure you're way ahead on prepping for the baby," he said, thrusting a bag into her arms and then setting several more down beside the door. "This is my contribution." He stepped outside.

"You don't have to leave so fast," Ally said, her confusion about how to react to this unexpected turn of events evident in her voice. "I haven't bought anything for the baby yet," she confessed. "I didn't have a clue where to start. You're way ahead of *me*."

He turned toward his rental car.

"Hey, wait!" she called after him. "At least give me time to thank you properly."

That was encouraging, Danny thought, but he didn't say it. "I'm not leaving," he clarified as he struggled to carry the huge carton containing a crib with all the bells and whistles. "I just went back to get this."

"More?" Then Ally tamped down her amazement and continued. "Danny, I can provide for my child by myself," she protested, hugging the baby store sack to her rounded stomach. But her tone did not so much suggest anger as it did gratitude.

"I know, Ally," he said as he leaned the box against the wall and shut the door. "But it doesn't mean you have to. This is my baby, too. I want to share in providing for him."

"Her," Ally reminded him.

"Let me take this." Danny removed the plastic sack from Ally's arms and picked up the other. "You said you weren't sure, so I got a neutral color." He led Ally to the couch and sat her down.

"I—I don't understand," she murmured as she began pulling things out of a bag. "A yellow receiving blanket," she exclaimed softly. "Sheets, towels." She pursed her lips as she rummaged through the contents of the assorted bags, then lifted her hands in stunned amazement. "How did you know what to get?"

"I come from a big family, Ally. Babies are no mystery to me. I have four sisters, six nieces and five nephews." He shrugged. "I was still living at home when the first few were born. I guess I sorta learned by osmosis."

"I had no idea," Ally said, her voice filled with wonder, "that a baby needed so much stuff." She ran her hands over the downy receiving blanket. "I had no brothers or sisters." She brought the blanket up to her face and stroked her cheek with it. "I had no idea where to begin."

"You mean you haven't gotten anything for the baby yet?" Danny hadn't noticed any baby stuff on his short reconnaissance mission through her house the other night, so he figured she hadn't gotten much, but he'd thought she must have a few things stashed away.

"No," Ally replied defensively. "I still have time—almost three months till the baby comes."

"Which will fly by at warp speed," he countered.

"What will you do if the baby arrives early? You won't have a place to put him."

"Her," Ally insisted.

Danny raised his hands in surrender. "Okay, I give up. For now," he added. "Until you have an ultrasound or the baby comes, maybe we should just call it an it."

"No," Ally persisted, grinning this time. "Her."

"All right, all right. 'Her' it is. Now, show me the baby's room. I'll put the crib together."

If Ally had any comments about that, she didn't voice them. She just led him down the hall.

ALLY STILL WASN'T CERTAIN how to think about this wonderful surprise as she silently watched Danny carry the many, many sacks and boxes into the spare room. She had planned to provide for this child. Why did Danny doing it now make her feel almost… guilty? And if she was guilty, just what was it she was guilty of?

"Where do you want this?" Danny said as he stood in the doorway of the baby's room with the large crib carton balanced on his broad shoulder.

"I'd like to have the baby in my bedroom with me until she starts sleeping through the night," Ally said, wondering if it was a good idea to let Danny Murphey within a mile of her bedroom. "But you can just put the box in here for now. I won't need it for a few months yet."

"Ally, Ally, Ally," Danny said, shaking his head. "What have I told you about being prepared? You're not going to be in any condition to assemble this thing while you're in labor, and I'm not gonna be here then. It should be put together now, while you've got somebody around and ready and willing."

"Darn you, Danny. Do you always have to be right?" Ally shook her head and rolled her eyes. "Okay, into the bedroom it goes." She followed him out. "Are you going to need any special tools for this project?"

"Just the usual," Danny said as he ripped at the huge staples on one side of the carton.

"Which are? I think I have a hammer and a couple of screwdrivers."

"Thank heaven for small favors," Danny muttered. "All the tools are supposed to be in the box, but I'd rather have the real thing than the flimsy, throwaway ones that come in the cartons."

"I'll go look for them." Ally, relieved to be away from Danny's potent masculinity, scurried away. Even though he had done nothing overt, just being in the same room with him, especially her bedroom, had set her heart tap-dancing against her rib cage.

And she'd believed that pregnant women lost the desire for intimacy!

But then, she'd gone without for a long time. Six months, to be exact.

By the time she got back with her small and inadequate toolbox, Danny had managed to wrestle the mattress, rails and springs out of the box. Now he was systematically arranging a collection of nuts, bolts and screws in neat little piles on the floor.

The room that wasn't very big anyway, looked—no, felt—minuscule with Danny, the crib pieces and her bed in it, Ally thought. With the baby there, too, would she be able to move around at all?

She handed him the toolbox.

"Thanks," he said, reaching for the tools without paying attention to her.

At least he was keeping his mind on the task at hand.

Maybe he'd be too busy to remember to grill her about her mother and her reasons, Ally thought. She perched on the edge of her bed and, hoping she wouldn't be called on to help, settled in to watch.

"You promised to finish the story," Danny said, though he seemed to be concentrating on putting the bed together.

Was Danny a mind reader?

"What story?" Ally lied. Danny wouldn't buy the idea that she didn't remember what he was referring to, but she felt she had to stall. The story didn't get any easier with the telling.

He gave her a look that told her exactly what she'd been thinking. "You promised to tell me why you are so hell-bent on continuing to be an independent woman even after you marry me."

"I didn't say that I was going to marry you," she countered.

"You will," Danny said with confidence. "It isn't a matter of *if* but *when*."

"If you know so much, Danny, then surely you must know this."

"Al-ly," he warned, his tone vaguely threatening, yet intimate.

Letting him into her bedroom had been a bad idea, but maybe telling her mother's story and, by default, hers would help diffuse the growing tension. Perhaps it would diffuse her urge to touch him, to hold him, to love him.

"It isn't pretty," she said.

"I'm a strong man. I can handle it, Ally," Danny said, pinning her down with his emerald-green gaze. "And stalling isn't going to make it any easier. Tell me," he demanded, crossing his arms firmly over his broad chest. "I won't leave you alone until you do. I want to understand."

Ally reminded herself that it was just a ploy to make Danny leave her alone, but she really did want to make him understand.

So, she began.

Chapter Five

Danny whistled long and low. He didn't like what Ally had told him so far, but he had to hear the rest. He *needed* to hear it. Needed to learn everything he could that might help him figure out what made Ally tick.

"Go on," he prodded. "When your father died, your mother decided to pick up everything and go back to Tamahlya?"

"Yes," Ally whispered. "She wanted to go back to the one place she thought she belonged."

"Can't fault her for that," Danny said. "There's a lot to be said for being around friends and family when you are down." He'd finished putting the crib together, and all that remained was actually inserting the springs into the frame and placing the mattress. He turned to give Ally his undivided attention.

She was sitting on the edge of her bed, her face looking pained. She wrung her hands over and over again, hunching her shoulders, telegraphing her hurt and tension. But as much as Danny hated putting her through this, he wouldn't give her an out. The telling would be cathartic, and the story was important to his future. To hers.

To theirs, he amended.

"She went back to Tamahlya to be with her family," he repeated. "Did you go with her?"

Ally shook her head. "I should have. I might have been able to help." She sighed. "I was a senior in college. I couldn't get away because of classes." She paused. "I didn't really want to get away," she added quietly. "I didn't want to have to go back to Tamahlya." She shuddered. "It's a terrible place for a woman."

Danny pushed himself to his feet and hurried to her, then settled on the bed beside her. He took her hands and covered them with his. "Come on, Ally. You'll feel better once you get it all out." He tipped her face up so that he could look into her wide, dark eyes, brimming with tears he wished he could stop. Danny felt like a class-A heel for making her cry, but he truly believed it would help her.

She'd been holding on to it for far too long.

Ally swallowed—gulped, really—and moistened her lips. "I didn't want to go with her. I'd been there before," she said softly. "I didn't like it. I felt as though I was stepping back ten centuries."

"Not exactly the kind of place a modern, young American woman would choose to move," Danny concluded.

"No." Ally drew in a deep breath and charged ahead. "Things had changed in Tamahlya since my father had attended the university there. The regime had changed. The *mullah* at the time was a traditionalist. No, he was—" Ally stopped and swallowed again. "He was a monster."

"Did he hurt your mother?" Danny said, dreading what he might hear.

"No, not directly," Ally whispered, shaking her head. "My grandfather had died since she was last at home, and my uncle, my mother's brother, had…had disappeared. That left my mother and grandmother alone to take care of themselves."

Danny wrapped his arms around her and pulled her closer.

Ally shook her head. "I have to go on," she said, her voice soft. "Of course you know of the Taliban."

Danny nodded.

"Something similar existed there, though maybe not quite as extreme. What few women professionals there had been were driven out of business. Women were allowed on the streets if they were modest and properly dressed, and they were allowed to shop and spend money if they had it.

"My father had left my mother well-off, particularly by Tamahlyan standards. For all practical purposes, she was a wealthy woman."

"Then I—I don't understand," Danny said, wishing that he hadn't asked. He didn't think he was going to like what he was about to hear. However, he'd all but forced Ally to tell her story. He would have to listen to the end.

"My mother found a lump on her breast," Ally said simply.

"Cancer?"

Ally nodded. "She knew what it was, knew what was required to cure it, but there were no women doctors, and she wouldn't go to a male doctor to get it treated."

"But there were doctors who could have taken care of her?"

"Yes. However, she wouldn't go." Ally squeezed her brimming eyes shut to hold back her tears. "She couldn't bring herself to be seen by a man."

"She refused treatment."

"Until it was far too late to do anything." Ally bent her head and buried her face in her hands.

For a moment, Danny held her to him while she wept. Finally, she looked up at him, her eyes red, her lashes glistening with tears. "Maybe if I had gone with her, I could have talked her into seeing the doctor sooner." She paused, then said dully, "In time."

Danny couldn't find words that would help. He could see how painful the telling was, but he still didn't understand why what happened had made Ally so determined to do everything on her own.

Ally's mother died because she had failed to do what she knew had to be done to take care of herself. For all he knew, Ally's mother might not have cared enough to continue living without her father beside her.

That was something they couldn't prove.

"You couldn't have done anything," he finally felt compelled to say.

Ally nodded gravely. "I know that. But I also know that I will never let any man, husband or stranger, or any society keep me from doing what I feel I have to do. I will fight to the death against any threat, be it man or nature, to me and my child. I will never, ever put a man's will, a man's needs ahead of my own and those of my child."

Danny was helpless to respond to that. If Ally had thought things through, she would have realized that a man hadn't kept her mother from seeking treatment; the woman's own personal modesty had. Still, these were Ally's feelings. He had no right to try to change them.

He could only try to make it better.

"I'm so sorry, Ally," he crooned as he drew her closer. Rocking her slowly, he rested his chin tenderly against her silken, shampoo-scented head and breathed in the fragrance that was so uniquely her. Then he sighed.

All he could do was be there. Understand. All he could do was love her.

And love her he did.

Now he just had to figure out how to get the two of them singing from the same page of the hymnal.

ALLY HATED HERSELF for falling apart like that, but at the same time, trying to help Danny understand felt good. She'd had no one to talk to at the time, no one to share that story with, and maybe by not getting it out, the wound had festered. It felt wonderful not to be holding that story in anymore.

As much as she'd been annoyed at Danny for pressing her into telling it, now she was glad she had.

And she loved sitting there in the shelter of his arms. Never had she felt more wanted and more loved than while leaning against his broad chest and having his heart beat so strong and steady against her cheek.

She tipped her head up to see him. "Thank you, Danny, for letting me get this out. I needed to."

Danny smiled gently. "I know you did. And it helped me see where you've been coming from all this time. I'm so sorry I made you cry, though." He wiped at her tears with the pad of his thumb.

As much as she loved being in Danny's arms, she was afraid of what it might lead to if she stayed there. Her emotions were too raw for her to be so close to temptation right now.

Ally pushed herself reluctantly away from him and forced an anemic smile. She nodded toward the almost-assembled crib. "It's getting late and we haven't quite finished the job."

"We?" Danny asked archly. "I don't remember you doing so much as turning one screw on that puppy," he said.

"I did get you the toolbox," Ally said in her own defense. "You couldn't have done it quite as quickly without it. I saw that funny little doohickey they put in there for you to use."

"All right, you win," Danny said, raising his hands in mock surrender as he got up. "I'll finish the job 'we' started." He wiggled his fingers in imaginary quote marks in the air.

"Thank you," Ally said simply. It was enough to watch him work.

She scooted back against the pillows and supervised as Danny put the finishing touches on the crib. Somehow, that piece of furniture relieved the awkwardness of having Danny present in her bedroom after so long. It was almost as if the coming baby was a tiny chaperone in the room with them.

Ally placed her hand against the growing child in her womb and was rewarded with the slightest nudge beneath her fingers. She smiled.

"All done," Danny said, stepping back to survey his handiwork.

"Suddenly, the baby seems so much more concrete, real, than she did before," Ally murmured, more to herself than to Danny.

He eyed the mound of her stomach, a smile twitching the corners of his mouth. "Oh, yeah. I'd think that growing stomach would have made it seem pretty damn real to me." He bent to pick up the discarded packing crate.

"Don't do that right now."

Danny glanced up, startled, but waited to hear what she had to say.

"Come here," she said, motioning to him. "The baby is kicking. Would you like to feel it?" The experience was so wonderful that Ally had to share it with the baby's father. This might be Danny's only chance.

His eyes lit up like emerald flares, and then he broke into a brilliant smile. "Would I? You don't have to ask me twice." He all but leaped across the room, and settled quickly on the bed, beside her.

Danny held one hand over her stomach. "Where? Here?"

Ally closed her hands over his and guided his hand to the spot. She held it against her tummy and waited, hardly daring to breathe, for the responding flutter.

The baby didn't keep them waiting long.

If the smile he'd gifted her with at the invitation had been wide, the resulting grin threatened to split his face in two. "That's it? I think we've got a little football player."

"Football? I don't want my daughter dressing up in shoulder pads and having guys piling on top of her."

"Now that you put it that way, I don't want that, either, but she could be a place kicker."

He caressed Ally's rounded stomach, and Ally had never felt so much in love with this man as she did at that moment.

"All right," she said. "We'll wait to see what she wants."

The baby stopped kicking and Danny removed his hand, disappointment evident on his face. "I guess the little kicker is worn out," he said.

Ally yawned. "She's not the only one," she said, glancing over her shoulder at the clock. "Oh my goodness. It's past my bedtime."

Danny pushed himself up off the bed. "It's past mine, too. Jake and I have been doing PT before class, and zero-five-hundred comes awfully early."

"Well, thank you, Danny," Ally said, wondering

how she could tactfully suggest he should go. He'd done so much. She didn't want to seem ungrateful. "Thank you for going to all this trouble," she added, as if he wouldn't know why.

She wasn't accustomed to asking for help, but after having watched Danny put the crib together, she acknowledged that she would never have been able to do it herself. Of course, she'd leave that part unsaid. "You didn't have to do this."

Danny stood there, the brown, corrugated cardboard box at his feet. "Yes, I did. How many times do I have to tell you that I'm a part of this as much as you are? I should provide for my baby, too."

Tears welled in Ally's eyes anew, but she blinked them back. Lately, she became a weeping wreck at the most inopportune moments. She needed to present a strong front now, not behave like the helpless female Danny appeared to think all women were. At least he hadn't said he wanted to take care of her.

"I can provide for my baby myself," she protested gruffly, even if she wasn't entirely certain she wanted to anymore. Not since Danny had marched back into her life and sent her emotions cartwheeling.

Why did he always seem to annoy her one minute and make her want to melt into his arms the next?

"I know you can, Ally," Danny said gently, his acceptance and his thoughtfulness still surprising to her. "But I need to. Is it wrong for me to expect to be a part of the baby's life, even if you won't let me be a part of yours?"

That statement, coming from Danny, was certainly not what Ally had expected. She'd spent so much time denying that Danny had had more than an incidental part in the creation of this baby that she hadn't really considered his feelings. Or his rights. And now in gentle but certain terms, he had reminded her.

Ally shook her head, too moved for words. And maybe just a little bit disappointed, as well. "No, it isn't wrong."

Danny had just indicated that he wanted her baby, but he'd said nothing about her. Had her subterfuge, intentional or not, made him change his mind about her? Had he fallen out of love with her?

Why now, after all this time, did that notion hurt? Was it because he was here, in her bedroom, in the handsome, fascinating, tempting flesh?

"We'll have to work something out sooner or later, Ally. You need to think about it," Danny said softly. Then he collected the rest of the packing debris and strode out of the room, leaving Ally wondering just how much she really wanted from Danny.

ALLY WAS LATE coming to class, and Danny worried what that was all about. Maybe she had been so upset by her confession last night that she couldn't make it to class. He hoped he wasn't responsible for anything like that.

Danny figured the best thing to do was let Ally stew for a while. He wasn't entirely happy about what had transpired last night. Yes, he had learned a lot more about Ally, and he was closer to understanding what made her tick, but he hated that he'd made her cry.

He loved that she'd trusted him enough to let him feel the baby move, though. He smiled to himself at the memory. That little guy—girl, if Ally had her wish—sure had quite a wallop for such a tiny thing.

In spite of that, he didn't seem to have gotten any closer to winning Ally over. He hated that Ally still didn't trust him not to be like Runt Hagarty, the one guy he knew who really did believe in leaving the little wife at home. Ally seemed to think that all combat controllers were Hagarty, yet he was the last person Danny would ever want to emulate. The idea of Runt Hagarty put a sour taste in Danny's mouth. He figured the best thing for him to do, for now, was to lie low a few days and try not to make any waves.

Instead of coming in early and chatting with the students, Ally quietly stepped into the classroom and called them to order right on time. She greeted them with a phony-sounding "Good morning."

"Good morning, Ms. Carter," he replied along with the rest of the group. She might have thought she had everyone fooled, but he wasn't fooled. He could see that she was still bothered about last night, and he hated that he was the cause of the dark circles under her eyes that showed, maybe better than words, how poorly she'd slept. How could he make her life easier? What could he do to help? He'd have to find a way that Ally would accept.

He blinked, startled. Was someone talking to him?

"Do you have anything to contribute to the discussion, Sergeant Murphey?" Allison asked.

"Sergeant Murphey?"

Danny shook his head to jar himself out of his thoughts. How long had he been brooding instead of paying attention to class? "I'm sorry, Ms Carter," he said. "I was thinking about something else." He'd been so busy plotting how he was going to demonstrate that he wasn't the narrow-minded man she seemed to believe he was that he'd daydreamed half the morning away.

FINALLY, IT WAS LUNCHTIME, and though Ally was aware that Danny had something on his mind, she had done what she could to avoid any personal interaction with him. Besides, she'd planned, long before last night's exchange with Danny, to meet Colonel Palmore for lunch today.

"I don't know, Kathie," Ally later told her friend over lunch at their favorite off-base restaurant. "Now that Danny is here, I have no idea what to do about it." She had finally confided in Kathie, and it felt good to have someone to talk to.

"When I first found out I was pregnant, I wanted to call him, but I remembered his attitudes about women's and men's places in the world. Can you believe he thinks that the little woman should stay at home and the man should provide? I didn't spend four years in college and the last eight years getting myself established in a career to give it all up so he could act like a Neanderthal."

"You could have told him about the baby, though. Didn't you believe he had the right to know?"

Ally sighed. "Yes, but I was afraid he'd insist on marrying me."

"And that would that be a problem why?"

"Because I don't want him marrying me out of a sense of responsibility because I'm having his baby. I want to be certain that he loves me for me. He has to accept me for what I am, what I do."

"So you didn't tell him."

"And I guess I didn't think far enough ahead to consider that he'd ever find out about the baby."

"And now that you have, you've had second thoughts about keeping it from him," Kathie said as she lifted her coffee mug.

"And thirds and fourths," Ally confirmed.

"How did he take the news?"

"Better than I'd have expected. He actually wants to be in the baby's life."

"I repeat myself. And that would be a problem why?" Kathie prodded, one dark eyebrow arched, as if she were watching someone or something behind Ally.

Ally sighed. "He doesn't seem that interested in me—" She stopped and tried to see what Kathie was looking at.

"Don't look now, but the subject of our conversation just walked in."

Ally glanced over her shoulder.

"I said not to look," Kathie hissed through clenched teeth.

It was all Ally could do to keep from turning the rest of the way around.

"Don't you know that the best way to get a guy's attention is to ignore him?"

"Really, Kathie, I haven't played games like that since junior high school." But curiosity was killing her. "Has he spotted me?"

"Oh, I'm pretty sure he noticed you. Something tells me he isn't normally a fern-bar kind of guy. Don't those combat controllers like to sit with their eyes toward the entrance, for security's sake or something?"

Ally nodded. "It used to drive me batty when we were dating. He'd refuse a table in a restaurant and make us wait for another one if it wasn't in the right position. Why?"

"He definitely isn't facing the door." Kathie chuckled. "In fact, he's got himself stationed perfectly for a ringside view of us. But..." She feigned a longing sigh. "I'd say he only has eyes for you."

"Should I wave or say something?" Ally asked, starting to turn again.

"No," Kathie said sharply. "Play hard to get."

"What's the matter with me, Kathie? One minute I'm mad as heck at him, and the next it bothers me that he hasn't come over to say hello. We didn't exactly part on the happiest of terms six months ago. Or the other night."

Kathie dug into her tuna salad. "Don't worry, Ally. I think TSGT Murphey is definitely interested."

Ally sighed. "I don't know whether to be happy

about that or not. I'm still not sure whether it's me he wants or just the baby." Of course, the way he'd kissed her the other night was an indication that maybe he wanted a package deal.

"Eat, Ally. You need to provide for that baby you're carrying. Regarding your Sergeant Murphey, let nature take its course. He appears to be a definite take-charge guy. I don't think he'll wait very long to stake his claim. And," Kathie added, "it's not *my* stomach he's focused on...."

Chapter Six

Danny wondered if Ally wasn't aware that he and Jake had come in. Surely she would have waved or something if she'd seen him. Still, it was fine to sit and watch her eat. At least she was taking proper care of the baby.

"What's so interesting that you let me have the catbird seat?" Jake said once they'd given the waiter their orders.

"Ms. Carter and Colonel Palmore are over there," he said, hoping that Jake wouldn't realize which woman was the object of his attention.

"Oh? Something tells me that it isn't Colonel Palmore you're watching. Should we go over to their table and say hello?"

"Maybe later," Danny said, ignoring Jake's assertion. He leaned back in his chair and crossed his arms. "Let them eat." There was plenty of time to make their presence known. Besides, he wanted to figure out what was going on with Ally.

One minute she was hot, the next thing she was as cold as a dead fish, and he wasn't sure he could chalk it all up to pregnancy hormones. Maybe she really didn't want to have him back in her life. Until he was sure, he figured the best thing to do would be to play it cool.

The waitress brought their burgers, and Danny tucked in to his without saying anything else. The good thing about his position was that even while he ate, he could see what Ally and the Colonel were up to. Too bad he couldn't read lips.

He'd love to know what they were talking about. From the animated expression on the colonel's face, he was pretty certain it didn't have anything to do with operations or the class.

He finished his burger in short order and sat and waited as Jake finished his. He wasn't sure he'd tasted a bite, but then, he was eating because he had to. Food was fuel and nothing else. Of course, if Ally were across the table, instead of across the room with her back to him, he might have enjoyed his food more.

Apparently the women had finished their meals, because they'd picked up their checks and Ally was digging around in her purse. When they got up, though, Danny concentrated on his plate. He didn't want Ally to catch him watching.

The women came toward them, and there was no ignoring the situation now. "Hello, Colonel Palmore, Ms. Carter," Danny said, rising to greet them.

Jake gulped down his last bite and scrambled to his feet. "Hello, ladies," he said. "Did you enjoy your lunch?"

"Yes, thank you," Ally replied politely, her gaze

studiously directed away from Danny and toward Jake. "I didn't realize you were here."

"Captain Haddad told us about the place," Jake said, making it possible for Danny not to have to explain why they were really there. No way was he going to let Ally know that he hadn't agreed on this restaurant here until he'd seen her car in the lot. "I can see why he recommended it."

Still avoiding Danny's eye, Ally said, "Sorry to cut this short, but we have to get back. Enjoy your lunches." She moved toward the door.

"What was that about?" Jake asked as he sat back down and reached for his burger.

"What was what?"

"That 'let's ignore Ms. Carter' thing you had going."

"Nothing. I was just being polite to speak to them at all." Danny leaned back in his chair and crossed his arms firmly over his chest, hoping that Jake would get the message that he didn't want to discuss it.

"Polite, my ass. Ever since we walked into the classroom the other day, you've been drooling over Ms. Carter the way a thirsty man in the desert looks at a mirage. What am I missing?"

Evidently, he wasn't missing a damn thing, Danny thought sourly, but he wasn't about to feed the man any more ammunition. "Eat. We have to get back to class. If we're late, it'll count against us."

Jake selected another fry, dragged it through a puddle of ketchup and shoved it into his mouth. "Anything you say, Murphey," he said.

ALLY REACHED for the phone. She'd picked up the receiver and placed it back down several times already, but she still couldn't decide what to do. She wanted so much to call Danny and tell him the results of today's ultrasound, but she restrained herself.

She still wasn't sure just how big a part she was willing to let Danny play in her daughter's life, and until she'd worked that out, she would just have to carry on as though Danny knew nothing about the child she was carrying.

She smiled to herself, though. She no longer had any question about whether her baby was a girl. Her obstetrician had confirmed the fact. And she had the printout from the ultrasound to prove it.

Now she just wished she had someone to show the printout to.

As if some cosmic fairy godmother had heard her unspoken wish, the doorbell rang. Ally hurried to answer it. She'd gladly purchase a hairbrush, magazine subscription or a piece of stale chocolate candy just to be able to share her photograph with someone. Smiling with pleasure, she flung open the door.

"Well, that's a sight any man would love at the end of a hard day," Danny Murphey said. He was still wearing his BDUs, and a glance at her watch told Ally that he must have come directly from class.

"Oh, it's you," she said.

"You were expecting somebody else?"

Ally's eyes clouded with confusion. "No. I didn't know who was there."

Danny narrowed his gaze. "Haven't you learned

yet not to answer the door unless you know who's on the other side?" He walked in, shut the door, latched the chain, then strode into the living room.

"You are not my keeper, Danny," Ally said, following him. He had to prove to her that he wanted to be an equal partner in the rearing of their baby, not that he planned to run her life.

Danny made himself comfortable on the couch. Didn't she realize that he was concerned about her? After all, she hadn't gone back to her office after lunch. The pool secretary had said she had a doctor's appointment, and Danny needed to know why. He cared about her just as much as he cared about their baby.

He had to be certain that he hadn't endangered her health, and by extension that of the baby, by upsetting her last night. She had seemed so tired in class. Danny hoped it hadn't had anything to do with him.

"You had a doctor's appointment. Is there a problem? Are you working too hard?"

The Murphey men had always prided themselves on being able to provide for the people they loved. Until Ally had raised an objection, he hadn't considered that to be a negative. After all, he'd seen how hard his mother had worked caring for eight children. He couldn't imagine her holding down a job, too.

Ally had started to settle herself into the chair across from him, but she spun around so fast that she could have given herself whiplash. "You certainly are full of yourself, aren't you," she said, but the pleased expression on her face told him she wasn't mad.

"I'm not exactly digging ditches, Danny. Of course it had something to do with you. You are the father of this baby, as you are so fond of reminding me."

"Is there something wrong with the baby? Is that why you had to go to the doctor?" Danny asked with alarm. Surely that little place kicker he'd felt last night was healthy and strong.

"Why would you ask that?" She regarded him as though he had suddenly grown another head. "Of course not. It was a routine appointment. I'll be seeing Dr. Schmale every couple of weeks for the next two months."

"Good to know," Danny said, releasing his death grip on the arm of the couch.

"She said little Ally Junior is just fine. I have a picture to prove it!"

Danny was so enthralled with the idea of a little girl having Ally's dark eyes and raven hair that he almost missed the second part of Ally's statement. "You have a picture? How can—"

She stopped him with her raised hand. "I had an ultrasound today. It's definitely a girl!" She reached for a sheet of paper lying on the table beside her. "See."

Danny could barely contain his emotion as he reached for the paper. This was something even more tangible than feeling the baby kick. This was a photograph of something that he and Ally had created. Together.

Out of love.

He'd expected a fuzzy black-and-white image,

but this was almost like a photograph. "It looks like a real baby," he said, unable to conceal the wonder he felt at what he saw.

"It is a real baby, Danny," Ally said, beaming. "Our baby."

"But how—?"

"Don't ask me. It's just cutting-edge technology that I don't even pretend to understand." She smiled again and crossed the room to sit beside him. She touched one side of the photograph as he held the other. "Isn't she beautiful?"

"Not half as lovely as her mother," Danny said, meaning it.

Ally beamed. "I'm fat."

"You're beautiful," Danny repeated firmly. Why did women always equate pregnancy weight with ugliness? He had never seen a woman as lovely as Ally was at this moment, her face full with the bit of added weight, her skin glowing.

"Darn," Danny said, suddenly remembering something.

"Darn? Darn what? You don't want a girl?" Ally's disappointment was plain.

Quickly, Danny gathered Ally into his arms for a chaste hug. "I'm happy she's a girl, but I was hoping for a son someday to share my Star Wars Collection with."

Ally eyed him skeptically. "The Star Wars stuff you had still in the original packaging that no one was allowed to touch? That Star Wars stuff?"

"Yeah. I can't wait to show it to him."

"But you won't let him play with it?"

Danny stared at her. Was she serious? "Of course he can play with it. Little Ally Junior can, too."

"Well, you didn't."

"You didn't come from a big family, Ally. You wouldn't understand."

"Try me," she said, pushing out of his arms and propping her hands on her hips as she challenged him to explain.

"In a big family you have to share everything. And you don't often get anything that is new. I started collecting those things when I was grown, to make up for what I didn't have." He smiled. "Now that doesn't seem so important anymore." He liked the idea of having a child play with the toys he'd only admired from afar.

"Oh," Ally said quietly. "You know, that does make an odd sort of sense to me," she said softly, and she leaned back into his arms. Then her stomach grumbled and the spell was broken.

"Well, there's no secret about what's on your mind," Danny said dryly.

"I'm so embarrassed," Ally said, scrambling away from him.

"Why? It's a natural function. It isn't as if it doesn't happen to everybody," Danny said, turning to see where she'd gone. He thought they had enough history that she shouldn't run off every time she did something silly in front of him. "Hey, don't run off."

She didn't respond, and Danny started to repeat himself in case she hadn't heard him. But one glance her way told him that wasn't why she hadn't answered. She stood in the kitchen doorway, leaning against the jamb, gnawing on her lower lip, indecision evident in her posture.

"Ally?"

She shook her head and yawned, or maybe she sighed, and then, standing straight, she said, "Can I offer you something to eat? You couldn't possibly have gotten any supper after you left class."

"I could eat," Danny said agreeably as he got up and followed her into the kitchen. "But don't go out of your way for me."

She crossed the small kitchen to the counter and lifted the lid off a slow cooker, releasing a fragrant burst of steam. "I tossed some stuff into the pot this morning before I went to work, and I haven't had a chance to eat, either." She reached for a wooden spoon from a crock on the counter and stirred the mixture in the cooker. "It's not fancy, but it's nutritious."

Danny followed her into the small room in three long strides and came to a stop behind her. He wrapped his arms around her and hugged her from behind. "Ally, Ally, Ally, you know I never was into gourmet food. Make it filling and hot, and I'm happy." He kissed her gently on the top of her head. "Is there anything I can do?"

Helping his mom had been a requirement in the Murphey house when he was growing up, and something about the moment reminded him of that. As a teenager he'd felt annoyed when he'd had to set the table or dry a dish; now it just seemed…right.

"I can set the table if you'll point me toward the dishes."

Ally smiled. "No, that's okay." She tugged open the refrigerator door. "I'll just toss us a salad, and we'll be able to eat in a couple of minutes. Go wash up."

Danny swiped a hand to his brow in a mock salute and hurried to do her bidding.

Ally shook her head, bewildered at the new man. Was it a real change, or just an act on Danny's part to get back into her good graces?

Still, she mused as she collected salad ingredients from the fridge, she liked this Danny as much as the old Danny she'd loved beyond reason. But she wasn't certain that she wasn't turning to him because she was overwhelmed with emotions as a result of her pregnancy.

As she retrieved a bowl for the salad from the cabinet, Danny came back in. She'd hoped to have the salad done and the table set before he returned. "The dishes are here," she said, indicating the cabinet. "You can go ahead and put them out. This salad won't take but another minute."

"Yes, ma'am." Danny reached around her for plates.

Ally hadn't realized that he was so close, and now she could smell his aftershave, and it evoked thoughts of steamy summer nights in Florida and Sunday mornings in bed. She shook the memory out of her mind. Even if she liked the intimate way they were working together in her compact kitchen, she couldn't let her feelings get the better of her.

She needed to do what would be best for her. And her baby.

Ally glanced over at Danny, who had turned to set the table, and reminded herself that Danny had more than a small stake in this, as well.

"MAN, THAT WAS GOOD," Danny said as he scraped the last bit out of his second bowl of stew. "Reminds me of the kind of stuff my mother used to cook."

Ally stiffened, and Danny wondered what he'd done to set her off. He thought he'd just given Ally a compliment. Was he missing something? He realized he still had a lot to learn about this thoroughly modern woman. He'd once thought he knew her so well. He couldn't have been that far off base.

"Danny Murphey, I have no intention of becoming the kind of little woman who waits patiently at home with the children, barefoot and pregnant, for the big, strong husband to return," she said archly.

Damn, he was going to have to learn to walk and talk carefully around her, but at the same time, he had to laugh. Obviously, she didn't realize just how close she was to that image at this moment. Try as he might, he couldn't hold it in.

Of course Ally bristled again. "What is so funny?" she blustered as Danny continued to laugh.

"Well, two out of the three isn't bad," he finally managed after smothering his chuckles. What with watching the various expressions skitter across Ally's face, saying that hadn't been easy.

"Two out of th—?" She looked down at her bare

feet, propped on the rung of the kitchen chair, and quickly curled her toes back underneath it as if trying to hide them. "Oh."

The look on her face when she understood what he was referring to was priceless, and Danny wished he had a camera to record it.

"You got me there," Ally admitted sheepishly. "I am undoubtedly pregnant, and I'm not wearing shoes right at this moment." She paused, then continued. "But if you think I'm going to wait at home for a man to take care of me, Danny Murphey, you have another think coming!" She glared at him.

Danny just smiled, and after a moment, Ally couldn't keep from laughing, either.

"All right, all right," she said. "I concede this one, but it is the exception to the rule. And I usually do a full day of work, as you well know."

"I saw how tired you looked when I arrived at your door." He held up his hand to stop her from speaking. "Now, before you go getting all hot and bothered, I want to have my say. As I've told you, I came from a very large family. My mother never worked out of the house, but she worked very hard at home. She was always tired, never had enough time. You might be able to do it now, but once the baby arrives, things will be different. Do you really believe you can have it all?"

"Your mother had *eight kids,* Danny," Ally pointed out reasonably. "No wonder she was tired. No way am I going to have anywhere close to that many. You can't tell me that one little baby will be that exhausting. How much work can she be?"

"More than you think. Just ask Jennifer and Rich Larsen." Rich had been in their circle of friends when Danny and Ally had been dating back at Hurlburt, so he assumed Ally would recognize the name.

"Rich Larsen got married?"

Danny nodded.

"And he has kids?"

"Just one," Danny said. "But when he and Jennifer first got involved, he'd just gotten stuck with his sister's two rugrats while she was in the hospital recovering from a car crash that killed her husband. Talk about a fish out of water!"

"Rich wasn't prepared," Ally countered.

"Maybe not, but he and Jennifer still have a hard time managing sometimes now that Sara is here."

"Okay. I think we're just going to have to disagree on this one for now," Ally said. "Let me remind you that I make a very good income, and I can certainly afford help."

"And leave the rearing of our baby to a stranger?" That was the crux of it. Danny didn't like the idea of a stranger knowing his child better than he did. And with him leaving for Tamahlyastan in a couple of months, *he* would be the stranger when he returned.

Ally started to say something but wisely snapped her mouth shut.

Danny pushed himself up. "I'll do the dishes, then I'm out of here." He reached for his stew bowl and stacked his utensils inside it.

"That's not necessary, Danny. Let the little woman do it," Ally insisted, her tone showing that she hadn't forgotten the original topic of conversation.

"No, dammit. I always pitched in at home, and I fully expected that I would do my fair share when I had my own family." He grimly scraped his bowl, rinsed it and positioned it the dishwasher, while Ally watched.

Then he turned, strode out of the kitchen and yanked open the front door. Without so much as a simple wave goodbye, he marched outside, shutting the door firmly behind him.

The sound of the closing door still echoing in her ears, Ally finished clearing the table and washing up the dishes. What had started out as a pleasant evening had fallen apart.

And she had been the cause of the disagreement. Why had she been so quick to take exception to everything that Danny said? Why couldn't she just accept what Danny was telling her at face value? After all, he hadn't said one thing about wanting to marry her.

Why couldn't Danny have just stayed out of her life and out of her business?

Why did he want only the baby and not her?

The tears she had been trying to hold back finally won in the battle of her emotions.

Chapter Seven

Her part in the current class was over! Ally thought with relief—or maybe it was regret—as she gathered up her equipment at the end of the day on Friday. She wouldn't have to face Danny every day for the remaining week of the course.

Irritatingly enough, Ally wasn't sure whether she was relieved or disappointed about this. She'd rather enjoyed feeling his green-eyed gaze trained on her as he listened to her talk, and his cropped, red head bent over his notebook as he studiously took notes. He'd really contributed to her lectures, and she'd appreciated the way he'd continued to handle Lieutenant Abernathy.

To think she'd been so worried that he'd be a disruptive element...

"Thanks, Teach," one of the younger members of the class called to her as he filed out behind the others. "I'll see ya around."

"Anytime," she called after him.

"I hope not, Ally," a familiar voice, low and dangerous, said from behind her.

It wasn't loud enough for the other man to hear, but she heard it.

"For heaven's sake, why not, Danny?" she said, now that they were the only two left in the room.

"I'd hate to have to fight him," he said simply. "He wouldn't win."

"And just what exactly do you feel you'd have to fight Airman Vucovich about?" she said as she picked up her laptop case.

"I'll take that. Don't want you to strain yourself or hurt the baby."

Danny closed his hand over hers, sending a tingle of excitement up her arm. Then he slowly unwrapped her clenched fingers from the handle of the case and took possession of it.

"You know very well what I'd fight him for."

Ally couldn't ignore the thrill she felt at the touch of his hand, even if she was annoyed at what Danny had implied. She hated that she was reacting that way, but she loved it, too.

Boy, she was one seething, pregnant mass of contradictions.

She started to protest, but stopped herself. "Thank you," she said simply.

There really hadn't been anything condescending about his carrying her computer for her. She was pregnant, and the thing wasn't exactly light. Maybe she should think about getting one of the newer, lighter ones that were out now, Ally mused irrelevantly.

She really didn't mind the little courtesies Danny seemed to offer so naturally. She wondered if that meant she was softening some on the idea of having a man do things for her. She smiled in spite of herself.

"Ha," Danny said. "I saw that."

"So? Even a thoroughly independent woman can appreciate a courtesy from a man. After all, I'm sure that if your hands were full or something, you'd accept my holding a door for you, wouldn't you?" To prove her point, Ally stepped ahead of him and leaned against the door to keep it from swinging shut.

"Yeah," Danny agreed grudgingly as he passed through the doorway. "Just don't let any of the guys on the team catch me. I'd never live it down," he said, but he grinned next, flashing his wonderful smile, so Ally knew that he was only teasing.

Truth be told, she would miss seeing him every day, she acknowledged. It had been nice, once the tension of that first day was over and done with. She didn't know if she should tell him that, however.

Now that she had been able to watch Danny over the past week, she regretted not having told him that she was carrying his child as soon as she herself had known. But it was too late to change that now, and apparently, it was well past time for trying to make amends.

Since that surprising, wonderful kiss the first night he was in town, when he'd confronted her at her house, he hadn't made any more overtures toward her. Neither had he done anything to show that he was interested in anything more than the welfare of the baby.

Darn it, she couldn't help thinking.

It bothered her. And it bothered her that she was so bothered. She was a woman perfectly capable of taking care of herself and a baby. She didn't need a man, she reminded herself.

Ally glanced at Danny, who was carrying the computer as if it were nothing as he strode ahead of her toward her car. It galled her to admit that she wanted a man in her life.

Not just any man, but that one: TSGT Daniel Xavier Murphey.

The problem was that she had just a little too much pride to admit that to him—especially when his knowing that might give him leverage over her that she didn't want him to have. Would give him too much of a hold on her.

She wanted Danny, but she wanted him on her terms. And not because he was willing to take responsibility for her and the baby. She didn't want him to feel obligated. She wanted Danny in her life only if he accepted her for what and who she was, lofty principles and all.

Was it foolish for her to want that, considering she was carrying the man's child?

Looking up, she realized that they had already crossed the parking lot. Funnily enough, Danny hadn't interrupted her thoughts. There had been a time when he would never have let a silent moment pass.

"I'm sorry," Ally said. "I should have had my key ready."

Danny stood by her car and waited for her to unlock the door. He shrugged. "No big deal. I can manage to hold this another minute or so. Or three hours," he added, flexing the muscles in his free arm.

Ally made a face. "Here it is." She fumbled with the key in the lock and opened the passenger door. "Maybe I should look into getting a bigger car," she muttered, thinking aloud. Maybe a minivan. The larger vehicle was sure to be safer for the baby and all the stuff Ally would have to carry.

"Can you afford the payments?"

"I can handle them, Sergeant Murphey," she told him quickly, bristling at the implication. How could Danny have reverted so easily to his macho prejudices? Especially after their relationship had appeared to be maturing. "I can stand on my own two feet.

"I have medical insurance, savings, a pension plan, everything. Believe it or not, I don't squander my entire salary on shoes and manicures." One look at her chewed-off nails would confirm that statement. Of course, Danny's unexpected appearance had been largely responsible for the shape of her nails this week.

"Dammit, Ally, I didn't mean it that way. I just figured you'd be worrying about expenses with another mouth to feed soon," Danny explained as he set the computer case on the back seat. "I could help," he offered, straightening.

"I don't need your help."

"Oh, yeah. You are woman. Hear you roar!"

His expression hardened, and Ally got a glimpse of what he must look like when he faced an enemy. Any suggestion of the good-natured man who had contributed so much to her classes was gone. In his camouflaged battle-dress uniform, trousers bloused smartly and tucked into his high-lace combat boots, he looked downright fierce. "Forget I said anything," he said, and turned and left Ally standing by the car.

"Danny, I'm sorry…" Her voice trailed off. There wasn't any point in continuing. Danny was already halfway to his own vehicle. He wouldn't be able to hear her apology anyway.

Why did she keep driving away the one man who might convince her to give up the notion of doing it all on her own?

DANNY HAD HEARD Ally begin to apologize, but he was stubborn enough not to acknowledge it. Besides, he wasn't sure what to make of it. Until he was certain he completely understood Ally's reasons and she understood his, they would not come to any sort of meeting of the minds.

He had the entire second week of the course to turn Ally around to his way of thinking. That would be harder to do now that he wouldn't see her every day in class, but surely it was doable. He just had to figure out the best way.

Hoping this wasn't a permanent goodbye, Danny watched Ally's car as she drove out of the lot. She was the most stubborn woman he had ever met. And he loved her.

Loved her?

That thought stopped him.

Yes, he did, he realized, wanting to reject the realization. In spite of two long years apart, and in spite of her deliberate attempt to keep his baby from him, he loved her. At times like this, though, he damn sure wondered why.

The car was long gone, and finally Danny swung into his own rental and headed back to the Visiting Airmen's Quarters. He still had nine days to work on Ally; plus, he had some leave saved up, so he could probably extend his stay.

One thing he knew for sure: he would make Ally see him as more than a sperm donor if he had to throw her over his shoulder, kidnap her and spirit her away. He was not going to go to Tamahlyastan without them getting every detail worked out.

Of course, if it were up to him, they'd make their arrangement legal, justice of the peace and all. However, he'd settle for an agreement that she'd accept his help in providing for the baby.

That wasn't his first choice, but a guy had to do what a guy had to do.

Danny swung into the lot in front of the VAQ and got out. He'd already tried out the pizza ploy, so he had to come up with something else. After slamming the door shut hurriedly, he hustled to his room to figure out Plan B.

EIGHT O'CLOCK and the other shoe had yet to fall, Ally thought as she settled in for the night. She had fully expected Danny to appear again on her doorstep with some excuse to get inside, but so far he hadn't.

Maybe he wasn't going to show.

Ally shook her head. Why was she so disappointed?

He hadn't exactly stood her up, since they didn't really have a date. But she'd already gotten used to him being there in the evening.

And as much as she hated to admit it, she loved the way his presence made her feel, as though she was part of a real family-to-be.

But Danny *wasn't* here, so she might as well make the best of it. She made herself comfortable on the couch in front of the television set, with a bowl of banana chocolate ripple ice cream and the remote control. Maybe there was a movie on cable that she could watch to keep her mind off the one thing—no, person—she didn't want to think about.

Danny, though, was the one subject she couldn't seem to stop thinking about.

Where was he? What was he doing? And who was he doing it with?

She knew she had no right to ask those questions in her current circumstances.

The television pickings were slim, and Ally dozed off. Sometime later the doorbell ringing woke her up.

Disoriented and yawning, she stumbled to the door and opened it without asking who it was.

Danny glowered at her from the front stoop.

She should have known.

"I thought I told you not to answer the door until you found out who was on the other side," Danny said as he marched inside, deposited something on the floor and closed the door.

"No, you didn't," Ally corrected. "As I recall, you expressed approval that I normally checked. That's not the same thing. And since when do I do as you tell me—" She stopped when she finally focused on what Danny was wearing. "What are you doing in that getup?" she demanded, still rubbing the sleep out of her eyes.

"I always feel better when I'm wearing the right uniform for the project," he said. Danny stood his ground, and the stubborn jut of his jaw challenged her to make something of it.

He was wearing what appeared to be a brand-new house-painter's outfit, complete with white painter's pants and white T-shirt under his denim jacket. A painter's cap covered his red hair.

Ally had to chuckle.

"I decided I'd help you get the baby's room ready," he said, arms crossed over his chest in a take-charge stance.

"Who said I wanted you to?" Ally wouldn't let him know how pleased she was that Danny was going out of his way. That he was here with her instead of hanging out, drinking with Jake Magnussen, at some sleazy juke joint on a Friday night.

Danny ignored her comment, brushed past her and headed down the hall to the small, unfurnished room that she'd planned to use for the baby once the child got big enough to sleep through the night. Ally scurried behind him, wondering just what he had in mind to do to it.

Flipping on the light, Danny paused and sized up the job at hand. "It's a pretty small room, but it'll do," he said, ignoring Ally, who was standing at his elbow.

"I'm so glad you approve," she said dryly. "May I remind you that I can do all this myself."

"Yeah, right." He turned around, fitted his hands to her sides and lifted her bodily out of the doorway so he could step back out. "And when did you plan to get around to it?" he demanded, his hands on his hips. "Until I bought one, you didn't even have a bed for the baby to sleep in."

"It wasn't because I couldn't afford it," Ally snapped, still tingling from the familiar feel of Danny's hands on her waist. And fuming at his statement. "There's plenty of time."

"Yeah, let me see," he said, holding up his hand and counting on his fingers. "According to my calculations, you've got two or three months. So let's just say, eight weeks. And I bet the reason you didn't check to see who was at the door was that you had fallen asleep on the couch." Danny paused. "You're not exactly a bundle of energy these days," he added gently.

Ally neither confirmed nor denied Danny's assertions, but she couldn't prevent herself from feeling her cheek to see if any pillow creases had given her away. "I was tired," she said lamely. "I'd had a long day."

"I rest my case," he said. "Now, either get out of my way or help, but I intend to have this room painted tonight before I leave."

Ally got out of the way.

"How DID YOU KNOW I was going to do it that color?" Ally wondered aloud as she stood in the doorway and admired Danny's handiwork.

He had painted the walls a warm buttercup yellow. Ally could imagine, as a finishing touch, a band of wallpaper trim illustrated with baby animals and chicks and ducklings prancing across it. Maybe she and Kathie could add something like that one weekend before the baby arrived.

"The room looks wonderful."

And so did he.

Danny had gotten overheated from his exertions and taken off the white painter's tee, and now his broad, muscular chest gleamed with sweat and the occasional paint splatter. Ally had managed to push the memory of his magnificent, well-honed body to the back of her mind…until now. How could she have possibly thought she could live without this.

Without him, she corrected.

After all, the stubborn man and the man with the hard-toned physique were one and the same. Even if Danny had recently displayed a thoughtfulness that Ally hadn't realized he possessed.

"Hey, the guy has more than one talent," Danny said, stepping back to get the full view. "My sisters thought that yellow was the way to go for a baby…"

He shrugged. "So, I figured in for a penny, in for a dollar. I might as well give the room the full treatment." He flashed her a brilliant smile.

Ally clasped her hands to her chest. And as much as she hated to admit it, she said, "You're right. I couldn't have gotten all this done by myself before the baby arrived. "Thank you for taking it upon yourself to do it."

"No thanks needed, Ally," Danny said. "It's part of my job…as father of the baby," he stated as if it were really necessary to explain.

"Well, I thank you anyway."

"Too bad I couldn't figure out how to work the *Star Wars* collection into the color scheme," Danny joked.

Ally didn't think it could get any better than this. And oh, how she loved Danny for it. "We'll wait till she gets older and then we'll redecorate and work them in."

Danny smiled then, a faraway look in his eyes. "Yeah," he said. "That'd work."

"We'll do it," Ally said. "I promise we will."

He turned toward her, an odd expression on his face.

Ally was about to comment on it, but he touched his fingers to her lips.

"Marry me, Ally."

Chapter Eight

"No," Ally said simply. "And you know why."

Danny hadn't really expected her to say yes, but he'd figured it was worth a shot. "I'm going to keep asking," he told her.

"Until you're willing to change your archaic view of man and woman, I will not give up my autonomy."

Danny stiffened, but he prudently kept any arguments to himself. No way would he do anything to send them back to where they'd been just a short week ago. "I want to take care of you," he said finally. "And our child."

"I do not need a keeper," Ally said firmly, her arms crossed authoritatively over her breasts. "And neither does my baby. We'd best drop this subject, or you can just leave."

"All right, Ally." *For now,* he added silently. He wasn't about to give up on his campaign to reclaim Ally. He wanted their baby, but he wanted the whole shebang. He wanted to make a family. Sure, her refusal had been a setback, but he wasn't finished.

Plus, he still wasn't done here. "Okay, now, go away. I have one more thing to do to finish this."

She glanced at him with questioning eyes. "What else could there be?" she said, admiring the room. "You seem to have thought of everything."

"I have," Danny said confidently. "But I haven't shown you the pièce de résistance." He picked up the ladder and carried it outside, leaving her to continue examining his handiwork.

"Oh, Danny, you wonderful, sweet, hardheaded man," Ally murmured. "I just don't know what to do about—"

"Here it is—" Danny announced as he came back in.

In his arms he carried a wooden rocker, painted white and complete with a buttercup-yellow seat cushion. "According to my mom, every new mother needs a rocking chair to settle her baby to sleep," he said as he placed it down next to the window. "With some baby curtains, you're good to go," he said.

Ally stood there, one trembling hand poised at her lips; she was too overwhelmed to speak. This was the kindest, most thoughtful gesture Danny ever could have made. And the fact her big, strong, trained-to-kill man had managed to accomplish so much in so little time simply amazed her.

Tears welled in Ally's eyes and she made no effort to stop them. She turned to Danny and flung her arms around him, pressing her face against his broad, warm, paint-splattered chest. "Oh, Danny," she murmured. "Thank you, thank you, thank you. This is so wonderful."

Danny squeezed her back, careful not to jump to conclusions. "You like it, then?" he said, gratified by her pleasure at his simple gift.

"Like it? I adore it!" she exclaimed, swinging around to survey his handiwork again. It did look good, Danny had to admit, even if he said so himself.

"You are my hero!" she cried, swinging back toward him.

"I aim to please," he said, loving what Ally had said and realizing that he actually meant his reply. To see the joy on Ally's face gave him an unexpected pleasure. "No strings attached."

Well, maybe a couple of strings, he amended to himself. He wanted the whole package—mother, baby and all—and he'd do whatever it took to get it.

Ally tiptoed up to the rocker, stopped in front of it and gazed at it again. Then she walked all around the chair, eyeing it from every angle. "It's perfect," she breathed, as she ran her hands tentatively over the smooth, white back.

"Maybe you should try it out," Danny suggested. He needed to see Ally sitting there. He wanted to imagine their child at her breast.

"Should I?" Ally asked.

"Oh, yeah," Danny urged. "I gotta see the full effect."

Ally pranced around to the front of the chair and plopped onto the seat. She wriggled her bottom around on the cushion until she was comfortable, then leaned back and rocked. "This is heaven," she said, her voice dreamy.

"Yes, it is," Danny agreed, not trying to hide the huskiness in his voice. And she was an angel, he thought. "Let me clean up this mess and then I'll get out of your way." If he didn't leave now, he might push her too hard and set his campaign to win her three steps back. He'd already pressed his luck with the blurted proposal. Still, she hadn't kicked him out.

Danny found his discarded shirt, pulled it over his head, then quickly gathered up the empty paint cans and drop cloths and hurried outside.

By the time he returned, Ally had fallen asleep in the chair.

"Ally," he called softly. "Ally, get up and put yourself to bed."

Looking like a sleeping child, Ally moaned and snuggled deeper into the chair.

"Ally," he said again, gently shaking her shoulder. "It's almost midnight. Time for bed."

She shrugged herself away from his touch. "No, too tired," she murmured sleepily.

Not wanting to wake her, and being a man of action anyway, Danny just scooped her up into his arms. As he adjusted her against him, Ally snuggled closer and murmured something that he couldn't quite understand but that sounded sweet and sexy, like sensual music to his ears. He carried her across the hall and into her bedroom. There, he placed her carefully on her bed and removed her slippers from her feet. Then he drew the comforter up to cover her and backed quietly away.

If she woke up in the middle of the night, she could get herself undressed the rest of the way—even though he would have been happy to help her with that particular task…

Danny started to shut the door, but paused in the doorway to watch her sleep. Unable to resist, he tiptoed back to the bed and kissed her tenderly on the top of her dark, silken head. "I love you, Ally," he whispered, tucking the quilt more tightly around her.

Then he turned, switched off the light and let himself out, locking the front door behind him.

He wished he didn't have to drive all the way back to the VAQ, but he had no choice. He was not going to take anything from Ally that she didn't offer.

SNUGGLED DEEP in the comforter on top of her spread, Ally awoke as the sun peeked through her bedroom window. She was still dressed in the clothes she'd been wearing the previous night, and for a moment, she couldn't imagine how she'd gotten there and why she hadn't put on her nightgown. Then she remembered Danny and the wonderful, surprising gift he'd given her. Smiling with sleepy pleasure, she lay swathed in her warm, quilted cocoon and relived the events of last night.

Oh, how she loved that man! And she smiled as she remembered his impromptu proposal. If only they could come to a meeting of the minds about that one deal breaker in their relationship, then her life would be perfect.

She pushed herself up out of the covers, found her slippers and put them on. Then she crossed the hall to the baby's room.

In all the months since she and Danny had made love in that hotel room in Florida, she hadn't really thought about being a mom. She had only dealt with her pregnancy one day at a time. She had concentrated so much on just getting through the pregnancy alone that she really hadn't considered the outcome. Maybe that was why she hadn't really begun to prepare for the baby.

Maybe that was why, by the time Danny arrived, she hadn't so much as started to buy maternity clothes, much less anything for the baby. She shook her head as she gazed at the cheerfully painted room and the comfortable rocker. She needed Danny in her life more than she was willing to admit.

Not because she wasn't able to provide for herself and her baby—she certainly had enough income for that—but because he would make their family complete. As an only child, she knew so little about children and family dynamics, and she no longer had her own parents to learn from.

She sank onto the rocking chair and leaned back. Still, until she and Danny could agree on what part she would play in any relationship they might have, they couldn't have a life together.

Feeling overwhelmed by the enormity of the amazing yet frightening journey ahead of her, she rocked herself slowly and cried.

DANNY SLEPT LATE. He'd worked hard at Ally's last night, and then he'd stopped off for a late-night drink to settle his heightened emotions.

He hadn't realized until he'd left Ally last night just how stressful it always was trying to keep from saying things that would upset her. That was why he'd stopped for that beer. One had been enough; in the old days, he would have closed the bar.

Still, his mind had been in such turmoil that he hadn't been able to get to sleep until the wee hours. Right after he'd heard Jake, who was billeted in the room next door, stumble in and run water in the shared bathroom between their rooms. Even Jake didn't normally stay out that late. Danny wondered what was up.

Late night or not, Danny needed a shower. He had washed up when he came in, but he'd been too tired to really scrub, so he hadn't gotten all the paint off. He closed the door between the bathroom and Jake's room and turned on the water.

Before he'd even unscrewed the shampoo bottle open, Danny heard the connecting door open. "Jake? You couldn't wait until I was done? Have a heart."

"Can it, Murphey. I thought you might not have heard the bad news."

"Oh, hell," Danny muttered, putting the shampoo down and turning off the spray. He didn't like the sound of that. Reaching for a towel, he steeled himself for what Jake was going to say. It could only mean one thing. "Who?"

"Nate Hughes," Jake said. "He was on a recon

mission, and the team ran into some insurgents. Lee Shoemaker lost a leg, too."

The news hit Danny with the force of a mortar shot. He bit back a curse. He had gone to combat control school with Nate and air-traffic control school with Lee. He'd been to Nate's wedding.

"Does Lisa know?" he asked as he stepped out of the tub.

Jake shrugged. "She's probably had the official word by now. We wouldn't have heard unless it was public knowledge. The mission went sour a couple of days ago."

He had been so wrapped up with Ally and their baby-to-be that he hadn't checked his e-mail or touched base with the squadron. Obviously, Jake had. "Will there be a service?"

"No doubt. Just don't know where or when yet."

"Probably Travis Air Force Base," Danny figured. "That's where Nate was attached before he was deployed. Don't guess there's much hope of us being able to make it out to California while we're tied up with this ops course."

"Not a chance in hell," Jake agreed. "But it doesn't mean we can't hoist a few in memoriam."

"I heard that," Danny said.

Forgetting about the paint, he dressed in his jogging clothes and went out for a run. It was too early to start drinking now, and he had to do something.

Sometimes, wearing yourself out on the track was the only way to forget the pain.

Even if only temporarily.

SHE SUPPOSED it was because of Jake's efforts, but this morning Ally, too, had suddenly felt the urge to prepare for the baby. She had been finding it more and more difficult to squeeze into her work clothes, so she'd decided it was high time she invested in some maternity wear. At least for work. She could continue to make do with the comfortable old clothes she'd been wearing at home.

Now, the back seat of her car laden with shopping bags, Ally, dressed in a new maternity outfit right out of the store, pulled up to her house, feeling pleased with her purchases. She was startled to discover someone waiting on her front stoop.

It was Danny who half sat, half sprawled on her welcome mat, his back against the door.

"What is he doing here?" Ally halted the car in front of the closed garage door and turned off the engine.

She beeped the horn, hoping that he'd come and help her carry her purchases inside, but he barely stirred at the sound.

What's the matter with that man? Ally wondered, annoyed that she'd have to carry her parcels up to the front of the house rather than drive into her garage. She'd have to go via the front door to let him in. But why was he still there? Was he trying to prove a point by making her do it herself?

Fretting about why Danny was ignoring her, Ally gathered up some of the bags and hurried up the walk.

Danny didn't budge.

Ally dropped her packages and nudged him with her foot. What could he have done last night after he'd gone that had left him so tired today? She shook his shoulder, and then she knew. The sour smell of alcohol hung heavy in the air around him.

She nudged him again, this time not trying to be gentle. "What do you think you're doing at my door drunk at three in the afternoon?" she demanded, not expecting an answer.

That last kick must have done it, because Danny stirred. "Ally? Izzat you?" he asked, slurring his words.

"Yes, it's me, Danny," Ally said through clenched teeth. "Get up. The neighbors will see you."

Danny pushed himself slowly to his feet, reaching for Ally, but when she stepped away, he grabbed on to the door frame for support. "Glad you're here, Alli-shon," he said sloppily as he lolled against the door.

Ally shoved him out of the way and unlocked the door. She was torn over whether to send him away or take him in and sober him up.

Option two won.

She gestured inside with a curt jerk of her head.

"How did you get here?" she asked, not really expecting an answer.

"Tak-shee cab," he mumbled, looping his arm over her shoulder and stumbling in with her.

Ally should have known. The military had taken a strong stand on drinking and driving in recent years, and Danny had apparently learned well. He was, after all, a good sergeant, even if he was pig-headed.

"We needa talk," he said thickly, appearing more like an unshaven good ol' boy than the sharp sergeant she knew him to be.

Ally shrugged out of his grasp, leaving him, swaying sloppily, in the middle of the floor. "Fine, Danny. We'll talk, but not until you're sober."

Danny looked at her, one eye open, the other closed. "'Kay." He lurched toward the couch. "Jus' take a lil nap," he said, and stumbled over the coffee table, landing awkwardly on the sofa.

"I do not need this," Ally told herself as she helped him settle onto the couch. "Go to sleep."

"Need a ni' ni' kiss," he insisted, puckering.

Ally backed away. "No way, lover boy." It was all she could do to keep from gagging from the stench of the alcohol on his breath. Her stomach was still touchy after all. "When you wake up, we'll talk."

She had a thing or two to settle with him, and she wasn't certain that kissing would ever be part of the equation again.

Not until she was certain this scene wasn't part of a pattern that might be repeated.

SOMEBODY WAS HITTING HIM on the head with a sledge-hammer, Danny thought with certainty as he reached up to defend himself. Then he realized that nobody was there. Not only did his body ache as though a speeding Humvee had run him over and dragged him a mile or two, but his stomach didn't feel so hot.

He tried to open his eyes, but the overhead light speared them like a bayonet. He slammed them shut again, and peeked out through the tiniest slit from the one eye he could manage to open. Where was he?

The place looked familiar, he thought. Oh, yeah, Ally's house. What was he doing here?

Then he remembered, and a shard of pain and sadness stabbed his heart. Nate was dead.

A man as young and healthy and strong as he was had died. Lisa was a widow. She had a baby to raise and nobody to take care of her.

Poor Lisa. Poor baby.

Danny struggled to get up, but his head weighed a ton, and he groaned as he got himself upright.

"Glad to see you've returned to the living," Ally said from somewhere behind him.

Danny turned to see her staring daggers at him from the kitchen door, her hands on her hips.

"How did I get here?" he mumbled.

"You tell me," Ally countered, her tone accusing. "I found you on my doorstep when I got home from shopping. You were out drinking all night, I see."

Slowly, it began filtering back to him. "Nope. Didn't start till lunch," he said with certainty. Actually, it was lunchtime. He hadn't had breakfast, he realized. Maybe if he had some food in his stomach, he might not feel as though he was in the third stage of death right now. "You got some crackers?" Anything to settle his churning stomach.

Ally pivoted so quickly that just watching the motion made him dizzy. "Don't do that," Danny protested feebly.

She came back with a plate of crackers and something dark and bubbly in a glass. "Here," she said as she thrust them toward him. "Don't think I'm going to make a habit of this."

Danny just looked at her, puzzled. He reached shakily for a cracker and raised it to his mouth. *Please let this work, please let this work,* he prayed as he chewed slowly.

Ally sat across the room, her forearms resting on the arms of her chair, fingers drumming impatiently.

God, that was loud.

"Could you please stop that?"

Ally did, but she clenched the armrests so tightly that her knuckles were white. If that didn't tell him her state of mind, the accusation in her eyes did.

He had to down all the crackers and half the soda to settle his stomach, but finally, he felt half human. Neanderthal, maybe. But then he'd have a long way to go to make it to Cro-Magnon. Danny took another sip of the cola and carefully swallowed it. It stayed down, so he swallowed the rest of the drink in one long gulp.

He didn't feel great, but he was alive. Danny looked over at Ally, who was still staring at him as if he were something she'd scraped off the bottom of her shoe. "I'm sorry, Ally," he said simply, truly meaning it.

"For what?" she queried. "For getting drunk? Or putting me in the middle of it?"

Danny shook his head. Damn, that hurt. Hell, he didn't know. But he sure was sorry. Anybody would be this morning. No, it couldn't be morning. He hadn't started drinking till after his run. He thought again.

He'd had that first drink at noon. "What time is it?" he asked thickly.

"Seven o'clock," she answered sharply. "You've wasted my entire afternoon."

At least he hadn't lost the day. He cleared his raspy throat. "I am sorry, Ally. More than you realize," he croaked.

"Danny Murphey, I'm so angry with you right now I don't know whether I can keep a civil tongue," Ally said, unclenching her hands from their grip on the chair and folding her arms over her chest.

"Nate Hughes was killed."

Ally gasped. She had met Nate a few times, a lifetime ago when she and Danny were dating.

"How?"

"Ambush. Lee Shoemaker lost a leg."

Ally covered her mouth with a trembling hand. She swallowed. Danny watched the convulsing movements in her throat and wished he hadn't had to tell her.

"I heard about an ambush on the news, but I didn't make the connection. I didn't ever catch the names," she said.

"Yeah. I heard about it, too, but didn't get the full story. Jake got an e-mail from one of the guys back at Hurby with most of the details. Not that it's gonna do much good now." He swallowed.

"We aren't gonna make the memorial service, so we had one of our own."

Ally seemed to want to say something. She drew in a quick breath but then she shut her mouth.

"Nate was married. I was at his wedding. He and Lisa have a little boy." He stopped. Nate didn't have a little boy or a wife. Nate was gone. He had nothing.

And Lisa had no one to take care of her and her son. Little Will would grow up without a father. Lisa and Will were alone.

Maybe, Danny thought, Ally would be better off without him. Then, at least, she would never have to face that kind of loss.

"I'm so mixed up, Ally," Danny whispered. "My head hurts, my brain hurts…my heart hurts." Danny watched her, trying to gauge her feelings. "I need you, Ally. I need you so much."

It happened so quickly that he wasn't sure how it happened. Ally was there. She gathered him into her arms and whispered. "I understand, Danny. I really do. We'll figure it out together. We'll figure out what to do."

Danny wasn't sure whether she was talking about his pain or their dilemma, but he didn't care. All that mattered was that he was with her, that she was holding him in her arms.

Chapter Nine

Lord, she had missed this man, Ally thought as she held Danny close to her breast. Even with the odor of stale alcohol still lingering around him, even with rusty, five o'clock shadow smudging his handsome cheeks, he was still the man she had so completely and hopelessly lost her heart to almost three years ago.

She had struggled to forget him during the years they were apart, but the truth was, Danny Murphey was the man for her.

Now that she was carrying his child, he was the *only* man for her.

In the years since they'd parted, there had been nobody who could compare. Nobody had even come close. Not that there had been that many, and there had been none since they had conceived their daughter.

Ally smiled. How much easier it was now to accept Danny's part in the parenthood of their baby. Soon they were going to have to start thinking about what to call her.

In spite of the message of death that Danny had delivered to her today, at this moment Ally had never felt more alive. Why did death always remind a person of the life they took for granted?

Danny stirred in her arms, nuzzling against her, his rough beard rasping against her cheek and only heightening her awareness of this dear, dear man in her arms.

"Ally, I want nothing more than to hold you and to feel your body so full of life against mine," he murmured. "But I can't touch you. Not like this. I have to go back to the Q. I have to clean up. Take a shower."

The idea of having him leave her, even for a short time, was terrifying. Ally clutched Danny tighter. "No," she whispered. "You can take a shower here. I don't want to let you go, Danny. Not even for a moment."

He pushed himself slowly away from her breast, and Ally could feel his reluctance and his relief.

"You're a lifesaver," he said lifting his gaze to hers. "I'll try not to let you down again."

Ally wasn't sure when he'd ever really let her down. After all, she'd been the one to end their relationship. She'd certainly let *him* down. He'd been the one who'd sworn to love her and care for her. She, not Danny, had been the one to creep away like a thief the night their baby was conceived.

Of course, they still had to come to a consensus on that issue of work. "You've never let me down, Danny. You've been nothing but up front with me."

Ally smiled gently down into his clouded, Irish-green eyes. "Go wash up. I'll be here when you're done."

Danny dragged himself out of her arms, but not before squeezing her to him in another heartfelt hug. Then he stumbled toward the bathroom, leaving Ally's arms feeling surprisingly empty.

Still, she had to smile at his departure. Even in a stained T-shirt and jeans, he looked wonderful to her. Especially now that she could no longer detect any scent of alcohol on him. His jeans clung like skin to his tight behind—from the rear, he'd *always* looked good.

Ally chuckled. Then she went to rustle up something clean for him to wear when he emerged from the shower.

THE HOT, STINGING SPRAY soothed Danny's aching muscles and throbbing head, and it felt good to be washing the stench of drink from his skin. Danny glanced around the bathtub as he scrubbed, and smiled at the collection of feminine items that cluttered the edge. In the years he and Ally had been apart, he'd forgotten how many things she used to make herself smell and look so good.

Of course, as far as Danny was concerned, Ally needed nothing extra to achieve that end. With her flawless olive complexion and expressive, dark gray eyes, she required no adornment. And her waist-length, raven hair was her crowning glory.

He felt a stirring in his groin and grinned. It

wouldn't take him very much time to recover from that stupid, though well-intentioned drunk. There was something to be said about being in top condition.

He hurriedly shampooed his hair with some overly floral shampoo that always smelled great on Ally but did nothing for him. He would be clean, and that was what mattered. If somebody from the team caught him smelling like this, he wouldn't care. He was so in love with Ally he'd risk the ridicule.

This woman was his reason for living. She was the thing that had been missing from his life for too long. His life finally would be complete if he could be with her, he thought as he rinsed the shampoo out of his hair.

But one terrible thought, one horrible doubt still nagged at him, he couldn't help admitting as he scraped at his tough, red beard with Ally's flimsy pink razor. He was slated to head off to one of the hottest hot spots in the world in just a few short months.

What if he didn't come back?

There had been a time when he'd felt invincible, felt that he could never die. He'd believed he could do anything. Ally had made him feel as though he could leap tall buildings, elude death. He had been certain that he was too careful, too well-trained for anything to happen to him.

Yet Nate probably had believed the very same thing.

Danny had known of the deaths of other combat controllers, but no news had affected him the way hearing about Nate had. He'd known Nate well, trained with him, eaten with him, slept in the same dorm with him. Nate had been as well-trained as Danny was, and that hadn't kept Nate safe.

And now that he himself was going to be a father, Danny was beginning to feel as mortal as the rest of them.

He put down the razor and turned off the water, sobered by the realization.

ALLY HEARD THE SHOWER STOP and grinned to herself. She well remembered the look, the feel, of Danny Murphey, clean and warm and slick from the shower. The scent of a freshly washed man was one of the most potent aphrodisiacs in the world, as far as Ally was concerned. Still, she had a sense that Danny wouldn't really be in the mood for love.

His body would be clean, and if he'd found the new toothbrush she'd gotten from the dentist last week and hadn't used yet, he'd brush his teeth, but it would be a long while before he was likely to feel himself again. In the meantime, she would get a good meal into him.

She lifted the lid off the soup pot and inhaled the rich aroma. Her mother had always said that a good pot of chicken soup would cure anything, even a broken heart. Ally didn't know about the second part of her mother's statement, but she was completely convinced of the curative effects. Chicken soup was one of the seven wonders of the world.

"I think I'm almost human again," Danny said

from behind her, and Ally turned to see him standing with one shoulder and one hip propped against the doorjamb. His rusty-colored hair was mussed and damp from being toweled dry, and he still had one of her lavender-colored guest towels draped around his neck to catch the occasional drip. A few droplets glistened on his broad chest; his crossed arms prevented any more from dripping onto his zipped, but unbuttoned jeans.

His shirt, light jacket and underwear were still chugging around in the washing machine, so she'd be treated to this enticing picture until his clothes were dried. Though she had scouted around in her closets, Ally hadn't been able to find anything that would stretch over Danny's broad chest without bursting at the seams. Sometimes being a petite woman had its advantages.

To know that he was being forced to "go commando" under his jeans because his clothes were still washing titillated her.

Ally grinned. "Maybe if you eat some of this soup you'll be even closer to human," she said. "Take a seat and I'll bring you some. Want some more crackers?" She ladled soup into a shallow bowl and placed it in front of Danny.

"Just smelling it is doing me a world of good," Danny murmured. Ally glanced around in time to catch him dip a finger into the broth and have a taste.

"Pass inspection?" Ally asked as she set a spoon and a plate of crackers in front of him.

"I'd give it about a ninety out of a hundred," he

said, scooping up his first mouthful. "Okay, make that ninety-five."

Ally arched an eyebrow. "Only ninety-five?" She set her own bowl down across from him and slid onto the opposing chair.

"Well, it is a little skimpy on meat," Danny said between spoonfuls.

"Let's see how your stomach tolerates that first," Ally said, tasting some herself. "I can fish some more chicken out of the pot for you if you think you can handle it."

"Okay. Whatever," Danny said, then polished off the contents of his bowl in short order. He held the empty dish out. "I'd get it myself, but I'm still a little green around the gills."

"Yeah, right. You just want to have the little woman waiting on you, that's all," Ally told him good-naturedly. She wasn't about to upset their applecart right now. They were doing so well, even if she should be really upset with him about setting up camp on her doorstop like a village drunk.

"It's damn good," Danny said. "Is it one of your mother's recipes?"

"No, I got that one from Mrs. Campbell," Ally said, glancing at the empty soup cans poking out of the kitchen trash. "I did add a few secret ingredients of my own, though."

Danny tipped an imaginary hat. "Tell Mrs. C. thanks from me," he said, spooning in more.

"Your appetite's returned," Ally said dryly as she watched him eat.

"Need my strength for later," Danny said around a mouthful of crackers.

Ally suspected she knew the "later" he was referring to, but strong constitution or not, it would be a while before Danny felt like his old self. "You want some more soup?" she asked simply.

DANNY HAD TO GIVE IT to her—Ally was being a hell of a lot more forgiving than he would have been had he been in her place. On the other hand, she hadn't exactly leaped into his arms. Although she'd invited him to stay and watch the video she'd rented, she and her popcorn were situated comfortably in the armchair across from him, her legs tucked under her. She had wrapped herself in an afghan as if it were a shield.

"Are you sure you wouldn't like to come over here and watch from the front row?" Danny asked, patting the couch cushion beside him.

"I'm fine where I am."

"I'm not. And you won't give me even a taste of popcorn, either," he grumbled.

"You know darn well why you can't have any popcorn. I don't think your stomach is ready yet."

Danny's stomach had stopped churning, but it didn't quite feel like the cast-iron fuel tank he'd always been able to count on. "Okay," he said, conceding defeat. "You're probably right about that, but I don't see why you can't sit by me."

"Because then you'd be tempted to eat the popcorn," Ally said. "It's for your own good."

"Suuure it is, Ally. I think it's because you never learned to share." It was fun to banter like this.

Ally threw a handful of popcorn at him, but it didn't make it across the room. Danny just shook his head solemnly.

"Too bad you don't have a dog," he said.

"What? Dog?" She screwed her face up in a funny expression of puzzlement.

"Well, I'm not going to vacuum that stuff up. If you had a dog, you wouldn't have to." Danny crossed his arms over his chest in a gesture of finality and then made a big show of turning his attention back to *Lost in Translation*. This wasn't exactly the kind of flick he'd choose to watch. He was more into car chases and aliens.

He caught a glimpse of Ally reaching into the popcorn bowl as if she might be planning to throw some more, but then she closed her little fist around the contents and lowered it back to the bowl. "You are so annoying when you're right, Danny Murphey."

"And you're so adorable when you're annoyed," Danny fired back.

That was apparently the wrong thing to say. Ally picked up the plastic popcorn bowl and threw it at him.

It found its mark, bouncing off his chest and emptying into his lap. Too bad she'd already eaten most of the popcorn in it.

ALLY WAS ENJOYING WATCHING him sleeping so soundly on his side on the couch, his arms forming a pillow for his head, even if he had left her to clean up the popcorn mess. It was probably her fault for picking the movie she had. She'd rented it not expecting that Danny would be there to share it with her.

She got most of the popcorn up with the carpet sweeper, no electricity required. No noise, either. Danny slept through the entire process without twitching as much as an eyelid. Ally guessed it was best to let him sleep it off at her place, rather than letting him go back to the VAQ smelling as though he'd bathed in jasmine.

She'd learned enough about men—and combat controllers, in particular—to know that he'd never hear the end of it if he came in reeking of perfume.

Besides, she liked having him here.

Had she really just thought that? Ally wondered why. Only a week ago she'd been ready to have him shot on sight. Or at least banished. Now she seemed to be softening.

But then, why wouldn't any woman want somebody like Danny Murphey in her life? Why couldn't she? After all, they had a history, most of which had been wonderful.

What was wrong with her?

Maybe she was just out of her mind.

Whatever the reason, Ally closed the house, covered Danny up as best she could, even tucking the end of the old lap throw under him to keep him snug. Then she turned off the light and went to bed. Alone.

Dammit.

DANNY WOKE UP disoriented. But it took only seconds for him to remember that he was in Ally's house, on Ally's couch, and remember why he was there.

A shaft of pain speared him as he recalled Nate's death, his own stupid drinking binge and the taxi drive across town.

Thank God, Ally had let him in and sobered him up.

He understood why Ally had left him on the undersize couch, but that didn't mean he liked it. It was cold under the skimpy throw she'd tucked around him. It was dark in the room and he had no idea what she'd done with his shoes and his socks, so he was stuck here for the night.

And wouldn't you know it—he had to use the can.

Danny got up off the couch—and tripped over the afghan that had wrapped itself around his feet with more tenacity than a landlocked octopus. He caught his elbow on the edge of the coffee table and muttered a curse.

A light came on in the hall and nearly blinded him. "What the—?"

"You woke me up, Danny," Ally said quietly through a yawn.

"Sorry. I was trying to get to the bathroom."

"I'll switch on the light for you," Ally said. "Do your business, then come to bed."

He wasn't exactly at his best at the moment, but Danny was pretty sure he'd heard what Ally had just said. It might have been a Freudian slip on her part, but she'd said it, nonetheless.

So Danny did what he had to do, then crept silently down the hall and accepted her invitation.

SHE SHOULD HAVE been surprised when he stumbled to her bed.

Then she remembered what she'd said while she was still half asleep. When Danny slid beneath her covers and pressed his body against hers, it seemed as natural as breathing. And oh so familiar. Why did her body crave him, when in her mind she wasn't sure this was the thing to do?

Ally snuggled closer to Danny as he wrapped his arms around her. She was so weak.

And Danny was so strong.

She should have pushed him away, but just having him there seemed right. What would it be like to wake up next to him every day for the rest of her life?

Heaven.

Just like now.

Ally wriggled around in Danny's arms so that she could face him, and she kissed him on the lips. He returned the kiss and pulled her closer, seemingly content just to hold her. And Ally was happy to be held. She loved Danny; she hoped Danny would be in her life and eventually in their daughter's. However, until she was sure of her final decision about Danny, she was reluctant to do anything she would regret later.

Then again, she wasn't going to get any more

pregnant than she already was, she reminded herself, as Danny relaxed against her and began to take deep, slow breaths.

Still wondering whether it would be wise to succumb to Danny's charm and proximity, Ally drifted off into comfortable, contented sleep.

DANNY DIDN'T KNOW when he realized he was in Ally's bed, but once he did he sure wasn't about to get up and leave. Here he was wrapped up in warm blankets, in a warm woman's bed, only inches from Ally. It couldn't get much better.

He drew her to him and held her close. "I want you so much, Ally," he murmured, thinking she was asleep.

"I love you, Danny," Ally whispered back. "I always will. That was never our problem."

He hadn't meant for Ally to hear his declaration, but now that she had, he felt fine about it. Especially now that Ally had told him that she loved him. But their breakup had never been about one or the other of them falling out of love. That would have been a lot easier to take than the real reason for their parting.

Ally shifted in his arms and looked into his eyes. "Did you hear me, Danny? I said I love you."

Danny squeezed her tighter. "I know that, Ally. And I remember why you left me. I just never fully understood until now." He kissed the top of her sweet-smelling head.

"Will we ever be able to work this out?"

"I hope so, Danny," Ally whispered. "I want to. You have no idea how much. Surely we can do anything if we just put our minds to it."

Once again feeling a stirring in his groin, Danny tried to push himself away. Obviously, he was not in the mood for any deep thinking at this moment, but now was not the time to confuse the issue with sex, no matter how good, or no matter how much he wanted Ally.

"Don't go," Ally breathed. "I want you so much, even if it is only for today. Make love to me, Danny." She pulled him back against her, pressing her voluptuous breasts and rounded belly against his aching, needy body. "Even if it isn't forever, Danny, I have to feel you inside me."

Danny would have shouted for joy, but still he held back. He'd never made love to a pregnant woman.

"Ally, I want to so much. But can we? Should we?" He swallowed. "Won't it hurt the baby?"

Ally ducked her head against his chest and Danny felt her shaking in his arms. Had he made her cry? Damn, he hadn't meant to do that. That was the furthest thing from his mind.

"Ally, I'm sorry. I didn't mean to upset you. I don't mean to hurt you or make you cry."

She looked up, tears glistening on her thick, dark lashes, yet the expression on her face showed anything but misery. "Thank you, Danny," she managed between giggles. "I needed to laugh."

Having a woman laugh at him at a time like this

should have been wilting, but her chuckles only made him desire her more. "It isn't funny," he said.

She pressed against his swollen flesh and smiled up at him. "You silly, silly man," Ally said. "I know it isn't funny. But there's no medical reason we can't make love. It won't hurt the baby as long as we're careful."

"That might be hard—" Danny stopped at Ally's sharp intake of breath. She pressed her head against his chest and laughed and laughed. "You know what I meant. Stop laughing like a hyena at my expense." Still, the desire was there. If anything, it had grown.

"It's just been so long since I've had the chance to make love to you that it will be…difficult to hold back," he told her, trying to explain without tripping over any more double entendres.

Ally took the sides of his face in her small hands and looked deep into his eyes. "I love you, Danny. I trust you. You won't hurt either me or the baby. Make love to me," she said. Then she kissed him solidly on the lips, displaying all the passion she'd been denying.

Thanks to Ally's sudden admission that she wanted him, Danny knew that the time had finally come. Besides, if he didn't make love to Ally now, with the assignment to Tamahlyastan looming, he might never get another chance.

THE SUN WAS HIGH in the sky when Ally awoke for the second time that day. She reveled in the sensation of the morning after, enjoying feeling so warm, sated and alive. Lying beside the man she loved with every fiber of her being was sheer heaven. She already knew that if he were to propose again, she wouldn't turn him down, no matter what she had to sacrifice. She leaned over to embrace the man who had made her feel cherished, adored.

"I'm so happy, Danny. I can never thank you enough," she murmured as she pressed her face against his strong, broad back.

He seemed to tense, and Ally backed away. "Is something wrong? Are you still feeling the effects of yesterday?" She was reluctant to put the reason for his "illness" into words for fear he would think she was accusing him. She wanted him to know that she understood the reason for his temporary lapse.

"No, I'm fine," Danny answered shortly.

"Good," Ally said. What else could she say?

He pushed away from her and levered himself up out of the covers, giving Ally a wonderful view of his gloriously male, naked body. He lifted one edge of the sheet and peered beneath the covers.

"Where are my pants?"

Ally sat up and looked around. His clothing lay scattered about the room, discarded before they'd finally made love. "Here they are. I think your socks and shoes are out by the couch and your jacket is on the hook by the door. Why?"

"I gotta go," he said.

"No, you don't. I don't mind if you stay all day."

"If I stay, I'll never keep my mind on what I'm here in town for," he said, softening his tone a little.

"I've got a test in Captain Haddad's class tomorrow. I need to study, and I don't need the distraction."

Ally could understand that, but she was a little puzzled by Danny's somber tone. He did not sound like a man who had just made love to a woman he'd been pursuing relentlessly. She leaned back against her pillows and watched as Danny dressed, covering up that magnificent body of his.

"I'll see ya," he said once he was dressed.

"Sure," Ally responded. If she didn't know better, she would think he was giving her the brush-off, not merely saying goodbye.

He'd been gone a full ten minutes before she remembered he'd come in a cab. Did the man actually plan to walk the five miles back out to the base?

Chapter Ten

The hike back to the VAQ base seemed like one of the longest Danny had ever made in his life, but he used the time to think, and the exercise helped clear his head. Embarking on this campaign to win Ally back had been so much easier when he didn't know for sure that she still loved him. When he hadn't been reminded just how wonderful it was to have her in his arms and to make sweet, tender love with her.

At the same time Nate's death made him realize just how much they both stood to lose.

Danny drummed his fingers impatiently against his thigh as he waited for a light to change. He might be on foot, but he still had to obey all the traffic laws.

The light turned green and he sprinted across the busy road. He knew that Ally could take care of herself. He always had known. Maybe her independence had been a threat to him back then. At least to his male pride. It wasn't really the issue of her working; he would have been fine with it if she'd been a grocery checker or a beautician. The fact that Ally had more education than he did and earned more had really rubbed at his ego when they'd first gone out. And he wasn't sure it didn't still, even if he was trying to see things from both sides now.

Had he somehow felt that because Ally didn't need a man to provide her basic needs, she might leave him if times got tough?

Was that what their differences had really been about?

Times had changed! Now he was genuinely happy that Ally would be able to support herself and their child if he happened to be out of the picture.

But could he put her through it?

Maybe it was better to lie low until after his assignment in Tamahlyastan.

Danny approached the guard shack at the main gate and dug in his pocket for his identification. As he waited for the sentry to wave him in, he couldn't help asking himself, Damn, why couldn't this just be simple?

ALLY LAY BACK on her pillows and wondered what exactly had happened here. Danny had been chasing her hot and hungry one minute, then had practically run the next. Her red-haired hero had always possessed a mercurial temperament, but this was mood swing to the extreme!

Still, she felt that she'd made some progress with Danny this weekend. She had detected a definite softening in his insistence that he be the man of the house. Even if he hadn't said it in so many words.

It was almost as if Nate's death had shocked Danny to his senses. Ally swallowed and blinked back tears. She had barely been acquainted with Nate, and she'd never met his wife, but the loss of any young man was a tragedy. And she felt so sad for Lisa, having to raise her little boy alone.

No, Ally told herself, today was not the day for negative thoughts. She had to think happy. Danny was beginning to understand. Even if he didn't quite know it yet. That was reason enough to cheer.

And since Danny had marched back into her life, she had suddenly become aware of some of her responsibilities as mother of this daughter she was carrying. Ally placed her hand on her belly and was rewarded with a strong, answering kick.

She smiled. "Yes, little girl. Your daddy may be a hardheaded man, but he's a good one." Ally sat up. "And we're going to do everything we can to make him see our side."

For now, Ally wasn't going to worry about Danny's odd mood when he left. After all, he did have to get through the class. Although she hated to view it that way, his life might depend on what he learned there.

Anyway, she didn't have time to fret about Danny Murphey's mood. She had some long-overdue nesting to do.

AT LEAST HE WOULDN'T be seeing Ally every day in class, Danny thought gratefully as he tucked his red beret into the thigh pocket of his battle-dress uniform and made his way into class on Monday morning. He still had some serious thinking to do, and until he could get a handle on what he wanted, he could do without the distraction of facing Ally.

He loved her. Of that he was sure. That had never changed, not even when he was so angry with her that he'd barely been able to function. He just didn't know what he wanted to do about it, Danny acknowledged as he slid into his seat next to Jake Magnussen and waited for the class to begin.

Hell, yeah, he wanted to marry her right now and make sure their baby had his name. But still the question plagued him: would it be right to give himself completely to Ally when there was a good chance that he might not be around for the future?

Jake nudged him with his elbow and hissed, "Get a grip, Murphey. Mr. Saloam asked you a question."

Danny looked up, embarrassed and certain his face was as red as his hair. He had to pull himself together. The last thing he wanted was to insult this new instructor the first day he stepped into the man's class. "I'm sorry, sir," he said contritely. "I was thinking about something else."

"It would behoove you, Sergeant Murphey, to pay attention. Is that clear?"

It was obvious that Mr. Saloam, the instructor, an immigrant from Tamahlya, wasn't going to be as forgiving as Ally or Captain Haddad would have been.

"Yes, sir," Danny replied. "Got that in one."

Too bad he wasn't as quick on the uptake with regard to Allison Carter.

NOT TO SEE DANNY in class every morning seemed strange, Ally thought as she worked through lesson plans for the next group of servicemen to come through the school. Though her material remained generally the same every session, she modified each lesson plan in accordance with the specific country the soldiers were going to.

She hated to admit it, but she found it hard to keep her mind on the task at hand. No matter how she tried not to, she kept wandering down memory lane. Though she was still a little puzzled about Danny's abrupt departure on Sunday morning, she smiled as she thought about waking up in his arms and what had subsequently transpired.

A woman could get used to that.

Ally glanced up at the sound of a tapping on her opened door.

"Well, it appears you're definitely thinking about something other than lesson plans," Colonel Palmore said from the doorway. "Whatever it is, it must be pretty sensational. "Do you want to go to lunch and give me all the glorious details? Or do you have a better offer?"

"No date," Ally said, picking up the scattered papers on her desk in an attempt to appear efficient. "But I'm not sure I'm ready to share the details yet."

Kathie arched an eyebrow. "Getting serious, is it?"

Ally sighed. "I hope so. At least, I think we're working through some of the problems that caused us to break up in the first place." She reached into her desk drawer and retrieved her purse, then pushed back her chair. "I could use a sounding board, if you don't mind."

Kathie nodded. "Always happy to help." She glanced down at her smart blue uniform with the carefully creased slacks and sensible shoes. "I might dress like a guy, but I don't mind engaging in a little girl-talk now and then."

"Well, I've got plenty of that," Ally said as she pulled a sweater on over one of her brand-new maternity smocks.

"Hey," Kathie said. "I just noticed. You finally broke down and got some hatching jackets."

"Hatching jacket?"

"You know, maternity clothes. That jumper looks nice. And long overdue. When I had my first, I started wearing maternity clothes at three months," Kathie said as Ally joined her in the hall.

"You were married to her father and had planned the whole thing," Ally reminded her, then quickly closed her mouth when she caught a glimpse of Jake Magnussen and Danny coming out of the adjoining classroom.

"Colonel Palmore, Ms. Carter," Jake said, nodding in greeting.

"Sergeants," Kathie said. "Heading for lunch?"

"Yes, ma'am," Danny replied. "We're gonna give the chow hall a try."

"Ah, yes. I read in the daily bulletin that pork chops were on for today," Kathie said, apparently providing Danny with an opening to invite them along.

"Too bad," Ally said, sensing what Kathie was attempting. She pressed her hand against her tummy. "My stomach hasn't been handling pork very well these days. Enjoy your lunch, guys." She turned in the opposite direction from the men. "I think we'll order off the menu at the club."

As they walked away, Ally yearned to hear one word from Danny.

"Later, Ally," he called after them.

That one phrase was enough to provide her with hope that she would indeed be seeing Danny later. Ally counted on that. After all, she'd gotten accustomed to finding him standing at her front door with some sort of surprise in his hands. Remembering how Danny had looked in his painter outfit and the thoughtful gift of the rocking chair made Ally grin.

"You'll have to tell me what that was all about," Kathie said as they set out for the Officer's Club. The Indian-summer air was balmy.

"What? Danny's cold shoulder?"

"No," Kathie said. "That smile."

"Danny painted the baby's room for me last weekend. And he brought us the most beautiful rocking chair to put in it," Ally explained. "The only things he didn't get were curtains."

"What's the matter? Doesn't the paragon do windows?"

Ally made a face.

"The situation is looking up, is it?"

"Maybe, Kathie," Ally said, sighing. "One minute Danny is the eager father-to-be, the next he's as skittish as…as I don't know what exactly," Ally confided. "And we still haven't resolved the women-working issue, which originally broke us up."

"He's scared, Ally. You've had six months to adjust to the idea of the baby," Kathie said. "He's had only one week. He's got a lot to process. He's probably worried about his assignment to Tamahlyastan, too." They stopped at the curb and waited for a car to pass, then crossed the street. "From what you've told me, he seems to be working through it just fine."

"I thought so, too," Ally agreed, recalling Danny's persistence at showing up on her doorstep. "But now he's drawn back a little." And it hurt that it had happened after they had made love.

"Gone to his cave," Kathie said. "That's what men do when they have to think. We women talk. They brood. It used to drive me crazy when Rob did it. Now I'd give anything to have him around, cave or not," Kathie added, looking wistful. She shook her head. "But going to the cave is a good thing for you, Ally. It means Danny's really thinking, not just reacting."

Ally sighed. "I suppose. I just wish I understood men better."

"Don't we all, Ally. Don't we all."

DANNY WATCHED ALLY as she and the colonel strolled off. He would have liked to talk with Ally, but on the other hand, what had to be said should be said in private. And he really wasn't ready to talk yet, anyway. Until he'd completely worked everything out, maybe keeping his distance was best.

But he could still look, he thought as he stared hungrily after her retreating figure.

"What's the deal with you and Ms. Carter?" Jake asked, bringing Danny's gaze back to him. "If I didn't know better, I'd think you had the hots for her." Jake hadn't been assigned to the unit at Hurlburt when Danny and Allison had been together, so he wasn't aware of their past relationship.

Danny was in no mood to discuss it now, but he figured he had to say something. "Just a little history between us," he muttered.

Jake glanced back over his shoulder at the retreating figures. "Must have been way in the past," he said. "Looks like she's got somebody else's bun in her oven."

Without taking time to explain, Danny hauled off and slugged Jake hard enough to send him careening into a light post between the sidewalk and the street.

"Hey, what the hell'd you do that for?" he yelled, balling up his hands, ready to reciprocate.

"Knock it off, you two."

Both men snapped to attention and saluted a major in service dress blues, whom they hadn't seen approaching. "Yes, sir," they responded in unison.

The major returned the salute. "At ease, Sergeants," he said, trying to conceal a twitch of a smile.

"In the future, though, save your fighting for the real enemy, not each other."

"Yes, sir," they again replied.

The major continued down the sidewalk.

"That's all we need," Jake said.

Danny's attention was on Ally and Colonel Palmore as they crossed the street a couple of blocks behind them. "What?"

"To be called on the carpet for fighting," Jake said. "What's with you, man? You were the biggest player at Hurby. Hell, you dated every single woman between eighteen and eighty. Why are you so hung up on this one?"

"Let's just leave it," Danny said, hoping he conveyed to Jake that he really did not want to discuss the matter with him. Now or ever.

Jake shrugged. "Whatever. It isn't like we're gonna be around here long enough to see the kid."

The remark smacked Danny right in the heart. Jake might not be privy to the full story, but was right. No matter what Danny did, he wouldn't be there when the baby—his baby—was born.

ALLY ARRIVED at her little brick house after work, realizing suddenly that she felt less tired, less burdened than she had all last week. as she drove her car into the garage she wondered why.

Then it came to her. She hadn't had to tiptoe around Danny all day! Well, except for that brief meeting with him on the way to lunch.

Had the stress of having Danny in her classroom

every day really been that fatiguing? Or had it been the evenings, later than she was accustomed to recently, when Danny had appeared at her doorstep and kept her up to all hours? Ally smiled just remembering Danny in that silly painter's outfit, covered with splatters.

That was certainly a side of Danny she'd never seen before. But then, she and Danny had never been expecting a baby together before.

Together. She liked the sound of that. Of course, the only thing she and Danny were truly together about these days was the baby. They still seemed of different minds about pretty much everything else.

She unlocked the door and entered the kitchen, fragrant with cooking smells. Well, she thought, they were sexually compatible, anyway. Once again, Ally noted that sex had never been their problem. She dropped her briefcase beside the door and went to check the contents of the slow cooker she'd filled that morning.

As she lifted the lid and inhaled the aroma of stew, she had to smile. She guessed she and Danny were sort of like that stew. As a bunch of separate and raw ingredients, they weren't much, but mix them up, add a little slow heat, and they were something.

Maybe they really could make a future together. It wouldn't be as fast and easy as dinner, but it was sort of the same thing, she hoped.

Anyway, she had to get moving. If Danny stuck to the same schedule he had all week, he'd be ringing her doorbell before long.

JAKE STEPPED into Danny's room via the shared bathroom. "Yo, Murphey. Wanna catch a flick? The last *Star Wars* is on at the base theater. Tonight only."

Danny looked up from the desk where he'd been attempting to catch up with the material they'd covered in the last week of classes. He'd neglected it by spending so much time with Ally, though he'd managed to cram enough yesterday afternoon to pass Haddad's test today.

He closed his notebook. He wasn't making any progress here, because his mind kept wandering to a certain instructor of Tamahlyan heritage and what had happened between them yesterday morning.

"Sure," he said. "I'm not getting much done here."

Jake rubbed his jaw, which was a slight purple where Danny's fist had landed. "I get it now, so I'll keep my trap shut."

"Glad *you* get it, Magnussen. I'm still not sure *I* do."

Chapter Eleven

ALLY ARRIVED AT WORK Tuesday morning, more tired and achy than if she'd spent the entire night with Danny, engaged in hot sex. Though she'd been disappointed that Danny hadn't appeared at her doorstep the previous night, she'd also been relieved.

At first she'd been happy that she hadn't been forced to "entertain" him, if you could call watching Danny work "entertaining." Of course she could, she realized. Seeing the way his muscles work was like watching a masculine and very arousing ballet. Once she'd gotten used to the idea of a brief sabbatical from Danny, she'd welcomed the opportunity to go to bed early.

However, sleep had been slow to come, and when it finally had, she'd slept only fitfully. All she could do was toss and turn and wonder exactly why Danny had stayed away.

"Good morning, pretty lady."

Happy to hear Danny's voice, Ally whirled to face him. "Hi," she said, maybe a little too brightly, in light of her bleary eyes. "I missed—" She stopped short. There was probably a good reason not to tell Danny exactly how she'd felt about his not being at her place last night.

Though for the life of her, she wasn't sure what it was at the moment.

Danny stood across the corridor from her, looking more like an awkward teenager on his first date than the confident lady-killer she'd always thought him to be.

"Are you feeling all right?" he finally said. "Is the baby okay?"

Ally touched her puffy eyes and grimaced. "Didn't sleep well last night," she said. "Sometimes I get to worrying about the baby…" She let her voice trail off. While that was not a lie, mostly she had worried about Danny's standing her up.

Not that they'd actually had a date…

"Yeah, I guess you might," Danny said.

"Yeah." Lord, it was hard making conversation in the hall and not really saying what she wanted to say. What had to be said. "I guess it goes with the territory."

Danny glanced at his watch, then made an apologetic face. "Gotta go. Mr. Saloam isn't as forgiving as you are about tardiness."

"Sure, go on," she said, though she wanted so much to grill Danny about what he'd done last night. Truth be told she wished she could shout at him for being so inconsiderate, not to mention causing her a hard night's sleep. But Ally wasn't sure she had the right.

She watched him go. Ally supposed she could

play the baby card and the guilt factor, but she didn't want Danny to think that she needed him to take care of her.

Yes, she wanted him—to love her. But she didn't want to tell Danny until she was positive exactly how he felt about her. If only he would say those few words that would tell her for sure.

DANNY STRUGGLED AGAINST the urge to watch Ally as she hurried to her office. He could feast on her image the way hungry relatives did a Thanksgiving turkey. Even drawn and tired as she was, Ally was beautiful, and he couldn't bear the thought of not having her in his life.

But, he reminded himself as he slid into his seat, he'd better get used to it. Tamahlyastan was a hell of a long way from North Carolina.

"I was beginning to think you'd have to get a note from the other teacher for being late," Jake said under his breath as Danny slid into the seat beside him at the same time that Mr. Saloam came in.

Danny shrugged. "What's he gonna do to me—make me stay after school?" Danny had to laugh.

Jake snapped to attention as the instructor gave them a hard look. "Lunch at O'Malley's," he muttered. "Ran into a couple of the guys from headquarters who wanted to get together. You coming?"

"Yeah. I heard from Chief Mullins this morning. They're putting together a memorial for Nate and wanted some input," Danny said, noting the narrowing of Mr. Saloam's eyes. "Heads up."

"Got that in one. Will it be square with your lady if you stand her up for lunch?"

Danny eyed him quizzically. "Why would she mind? I don't have to answer to her. She's not my lady," he lied.

"Yeah right, man. And I'm not a tech sergeant in the United States Air Force."

The instructor slammed a book down on the desk, and Danny figured it would be best to give the man his full attention.

Even if Ally Carter was the only instructor at this specialty school he really wanted to focus on.

ONE OF THE ADVANTAGES of having an office adjoining the classroom Danny was in was that Ally could see through the rippled-glass window in her door and knew exactly when Danny's class adjourned. She had packed some leftover stew from supper last night. She could heat it in the office microwave if her plan didn't work out; however, she had every intention of waylaying Sergeant Danny Murphey and finding out what was on his mind. If she had to buy him lunch, she could certainly afford it.

She had managed to accomplish a good bit of planning this morning in spite of her less-than-satisfactory night's sleep. Of course, she hadn't gotten much done on her lesson plans.

She had figured out a script for what she would say when she next saw Danny Murphey. And if that didn't work out, she knew what else she had to do. Ally smiled as she thought about step two.

She saw Mr. Saloam dismiss the class through the window in the door. Good. Mr. Saloam was nothing if not scheduled. Ally put down the pencil she hadn't really been using and grabbed for her purse. All she had to do was be in the hallway as Danny and the rest of the class walked out.

Smiling, Ally stepped into the hall. To be in charge for a change felt good. She was so focused on congratulating herself that she almost collided with the object of her campaign.

"Oh, Danny. I didn't see you there." It was the truth. Even if she had planned to run into him in the hall, she hadn't intended to do it physically.

"Sorry, Ms. Carter." Danny was always conscientious about protocol when they were in public. "I was in a hurry to meet some buddies from HQ, so I wasn't looking."

"You have plans?" Ally tried not to let him know how disappointed she was. "Thought I might talk you into joining me at the snack bar," she added. "Colonel Palmore is tied up with a planning conference for the rest of this week, and I hate to eat alone."

"Actually," Jake Magnussen said, "we're meeting to plan a memorial for Nate Hughes."

"I was so sorry to hear about him. I remember him from Hurlburt, though I never met his wife."

"Yeah, it's always tough on the family," Danny interjected gruffly. "Hey, we gotta make tracks or we won't get back in time."

"I sure hope Lisa has some job experience to help

her get by," Ally said quietly, trying not-so-subtly to make a point while she could.

Danny and Jake hurried down the corridor, and Ally enjoyed the view of their hasty retreat. Of course, baggy, multipocketed battle-dress uniforms weren't as revealing as skintight jeans, but there was something about the confident way the two men walked that had her attention.

When the exterior door closed behind them, Ally turned back toward her office to eat her meal alone.

Even though lunch hadn't gone exactly as she'd planned, she still had that other idea she could put into action. It might not exactly be on the up-and-up, but Ally liked it.

"Yesss!" she cheered as she reached into her desk drawer for the backup lunch she'd packed. Tonight's campaign was going to work.

It had to.

DANNY'S MIND wasn't really on the conversation over steaks and beer at the off-base steakhouse. Something about Ally's parting shot nagged at him. He wondered what she meant with that remark about jobs to fall back on. Then after a moment he understood.

For the first time in his life, he was beginning to see the other side. His father may have worked two, sometimes three jobs to keep his mother from having to seek employment, but he'd never really had the time to enjoy the life and family he'd built. When he'd died suddenly and much too young, Danny's mother had been totally unprepared to support the two kids still at home. In fact, that was when Danny had abandoned his college plans and joined the Air Force, to keep her from having his mouth to feed, as well, even though he hadn't expected her to pay his tuition.

"Talk about a guy being in the middle of things. Three big skirmishes and still not a mark on him."

Danny shook his head. "Who's this? I thought we were supposed to be planning a memorial service."

"Beam me up, Scotty. There's no intelligent life here." Chief Mullins took another swig of his beer and then he grinned. "Nah, that's already taken care of. We just wanted to figure out a way to be sure you'd be here."

Okay, maybe he had been thinking about Ally, but usually he wasn't that slow on the uptake. "What for?"

"Do we need a reason?" Senior Master Sergeant Jones asked.

"Just wanted to get away from all those suit-and-tie guys and back with some real men," Chief Mullins said, tugging at his dark blue uniform tie. The chief had been promoted to headquarters, but he made no secret that he preferred the action of the trenches.

"Got that in one," Jake said.

Danny raised his hands in a confused gesture. "Okay, I admit I was zoned out, but who the hell are you talking about?"

"Vic Valentino," Jones supplied.

"Don't know the man," Danny said. "What about him?"

"He's up for his third bronze star. Been in three major skirmishes in two assignments and got out without a single scratch. He was there when Nate bought it. Was the one to field-dress Shoemaker's injury. Probably saved his life."

Chief Mullins filled him in some more. "Yeah, he's at the end of his tour and he's slated for Hurby. You'll probably run into him before you head off for Tamahlyastan. Do you some good to talk to him before you go."

"Yeah," SMSGT Jones agreed. "You'll damn sure get more useful information from him than you ever will from two weeks in class here."

"Heard that," Jake said, lifting his long-neck.

"Got it," Danny said. Maybe he would look Valentino up when he got back to Hurlburt. He wanted all the advice he could get to make sure he returned all in one piece.

After all, he did have someone—make that two people—to come back for.

Too bad Valentino couldn't tell him how to deal with Allison Raneea Carter, Danny couldn't help thinking as he raised his own bottle in an unspoken toast.

CAPTAIN HADDAD had mentioned that his Dachshund had just had a litter. Ally rubbed her hands together with delight. How could Danny possibly resist her request? After all, he'd been the one to bring up getting a dog.

This time Ally posted herself in the hall. She didn't have to pretend that she was running in to Danny. She was going to make a direct request, so if she looked as though she was waiting for him, no big deal.

It seemed to take forever for the class to end, but finally she heard the scuffle of chairs and the chatter of voices, signaling the end of the day. Ally positioned herself just outside the classroom door, not in the way, but near enough to grab Danny as he went by.

The door opened and students hurried out, but Danny wasn't among them. Wouldn't you know that he'd be the one to linger after class.

She could almost believe that Danny was trying to avoid her.

Then he stepped out, deep in conversation with Captain Haddad, who still taught the afternoon session. It couldn't have worked out better if she'd planned it that way. "Oh! Hi, Danny. Could I have a word with you for a moment?"

Danny looked up, startled. Since she was no longer his teacher, he probably thought he'd have to explain their relationship to the captain.

"Yes, ma'am?"

"You can drop the act, Danny. The secret will be out after tonight anyway."

Captain Haddad looked as though he wanted to run away, and Danny looked downright panicky. "What secret?"

"Why the puppy, of course." She batted her eyelashes at the captain in a thoroughly un-Ally-like manner. Then she turned to Danny. "Captain Haddad has a litter of Dachshund puppies he's selling. Since you suggested I get a dog the other night, I thought I'd get your advice when I pick one out."

The look on Danny's face was priceless. Clearly, he didn't know whether to deny any knowledge of what she was talking about or to simply smile and nod accordingly.

Ally figured she'd best give Danny an out to allow him to save face. "Danny and I are old friends from Hurlburt Field," she explained. "He suggested that I ought to have a dog," she added, without clarifying how the subject had come up.

"Don't you want something a little bigger than a Dachshund for protection?" the captain asked.

"No, I'm a small woman, and I don't want a killer guard dog around my baby," she said, placing her hand protectively over her stomach. "Besides, I don't want a dog for protection. Just company." She paused. "What do you say, Danny?"

Damn, Danny thought. How did she do that? He'd just been talking to Haddad about the puppies. She might have ruined the surprise, but at least, he could go along with her request. "Sure, I'll help you pick one out."

Besides, if they were at Captain Haddad's place, they wouldn't be tempted to do something it really wasn't a good idea to do. Not until they'd sorted out the technicalities.

Captain Haddad looked back and forth between

them, seemingly trying to figure out exactly what was going on. He might know that they were "friends" from Hurlburt, but he didn't know about their other connection. "Do you want to come by tonight after dinner?"

Danny glanced at Ally—not a difficult task any time. "That okay with you?"

Ally nodded, as smug as a fat cat with feathers on her lips. "Perfect. And I'll be happy to fix supper for you to thank you for your help," she said.

"You don't have to," Danny protested. "Let me take you out. It'll be easier for both of us."

Boy, he was smooth. He'd just asked Ally for a date, in front of a witness, no less, and she hadn't been able to refuse. On top of that, because she'd been the one to ask him to see a puppy that Haddad had for sale, Ally had a reason for being seen in public with him.

Pretty cool, if he hadn't really thought of the idea himself.

"Then, I'll pay," Ally insisted. "After all, you're doing a favor for me."

Did she always have to insist on paying? Danny smiled grimly. "Sure, Ally. I'll pick you up."

Ally clapped her hands with delight. "Wonderful." She looked at the captain. "What time would be convenient for you?"

The captain suggested a time.

"Great. We'll see you there." Then Ally looped her arm through Danny's and steered him in the opposite direction.

"What the hell was that all about?" Danny demanded as soon as he was sure they were out of earshot.

Ally stopped, her gray eyes wide with…innocence? "What was what? You suggested that I needed a dog, so I'm getting one."

"Cut it out, Ally. You have never been a dog person. What's the deal?"

"No deal. I thought our daughter might like to have a puppy. I want a puppy." She chuckled. "It's getting harder and harder to bring myself to pull out the vacuum cleaner in the evenings after a hard day's work."

Danny had to smile. "Yeah, right."

Plainly, Ally had made an excuse to spend time with him.

Subterfuge or not, Danny didn't mind at all.

WHILE ALLY WAITED for Danny to arrive, she took a few minutes to freshen up. She smiled into the bathroom mirror.

"Perfect," she told her reflection. The baby seemed to agree, giving her a swift kick. "Yes, sweetie. I know you're hungry. We'll get us something good to eat in just a few minutes. Just as soon as your daddy gets here."

Of course Danny had insisted upon driving, though he had never been to Roger Haddad's house. That was her man-of-the-house Danny, all right. Many times she loved his confident attitude. Of course, there had been other times when she wasn't quite as thrilled.

She really needed his undivided attention. They'd be alone in the car and at the restaurant, but they wouldn't be able to talk. They ought to be completely alone, away from listening ears. That would be harder to arrange.

Or would it?

She would require his help getting the puppy settled in. She smiled again. This was just getting better and better.

The doorbell rang, and Ally quickly finished her primping, even spritzing herself with a generous amount of the expensive, jasmine-scented perfume she saved for special occasions. Seducing Danny Murphey certainly counted as one of those.

She couldn't wait to get on with step two of her master plan.

Taking one last check in the full-length mirror in the hall, Ally had to admit she looked great. Even for a short pregnant lady, she looked pretty good. Then she thought of one last, perfect touch.

She pulled the pins out of her sensible twist and let her hair swing free. Danny always had loved her hair loose. She ran her fingers through it to tousle it, then admired the results. "Dynamite," she said.

Ally hurried to the door and reached for the handle. Remembering Danny's previous warnings about not opening doors without finding out who was behind them, she held herself back. "Who is it?" she called in a saccharine voice.

"Come off it, Ally. You know damn well who it is," Danny answered.

Ally flung open the door. "Well, you did tell me not to open the door till I knew who was there," she reminded him. She certainly was enjoying this. If she had to pretend to be a helpless ninny to catch her man, she would.

After all, Technical Sergeant Daniel X. Murphey was certainly worth it. Ally beamed up into his glowering face, and enjoyed watching his frown turn to an admiring grin.

"Wow. You look hot!" Danny declared.

"Thanks," Ally replied, pleased she had gotten exactly the reaction she'd wanted. There was something about long hair cascading around a woman's shoulders that always turned guys on. And she wasn't above using all the tools at her disposal tonight. "Are you ready? We're starved."

Danny glanced around as if expecting to find someone lurking in the shadows. "We? Who's going with us?"

"The *baby* and I, Danny. Like I said, we're very hungry." *And me—I'm hungry for you.* "Ready to go? If we don't get going, we'll end up keeping Roger waiting."

"Can't let that happen," Danny said, crooking his arm.

Ally accepted it gladly and followed Danny out the door.

"It's not every day that I get to take my two best girls out to dinner."

"But remember, I'm paying," Ally said as she closed and locked the front door.

"Can we renegotiate?"

"Why? Dinner was my idea. Besides, if I pay, I get to choose the restaurant," she said. "I know the perfect place."

Danny lifted his hands, feigning surrender. "I give up. You win. Just please don't make me eat in one of those froufrou places where they serve alfalfa sprout-and-tofu sandwiches. A guy could starve to death before he got out of a place like that."

"Who do you think you're dealing with here?" Ally said as Danny opened the passenger door for her. "I want red meat. And I want lots of it. I think you'll approve of the place I have in mind." Ally settled into the seat and reached for her seat belt. "Now, come on. The native is getting restless." She folded her hands across her stomach and was rewarded with a healthy nudge. "Ally Junior is hungry."

Danny swung into the car. "Lead on, Ms. Carter. Since I don't know where we're going, you can be the navigator." He belted himself in and started the car. "Oh, and we are gonna have to discuss names. Tonight is as good a time as any to start."

Ally didn't respond. She just grinned.

Everything was falling right into place.

Chapter Twelve

Danny sat back and watched Ally as she perused the menu at O'Malley's. He didn't have the heart to tell her that he'd been there for lunch today, but then, did it matter? He himself couldn't have picked a better place.

"I'm so hungry I could eat a side of beef single-handedly," Ally said as she continued to scan the menu. She read each entry with deep concentration, her tongue tucked in the side of her mouth, occasionally flicking back and forth to moisten her lips.

Holy Toledo, Danny realized, she could get him worked up without even trying. If they didn't settle their differences soon, Danny would be a complete basket case. "I'm pretty hungry myself," he said, more as a way to distract himself than anything else. He'd already made his decision. On his entree…and Ally.

"Okay, I've finally decided," Ally said, snapping her menu shut. "How 'bout you?"

"Oh, yeah," Danny said. "I know exactly what I

want." He wanted Ally now and forever. How to get her was still the crux of the problem. "I'm going to have the New York strip."

"Good choice," Ally declared. "That's a little big for me. I'll have a filet mignon. And a really, really big baked potato with all the trimmings."

"Only a filet mignon? I thought you were hungry enough to eat a horse."

Ally made a shocked face. "I could never eat Black Beauty."

Danny had to laugh. "I was speaking figuratively, of course. You're making up for it with the loaded potato, you realize."

The dining room was crowded, so Ally lowered her voice. She looked at him conspiratorially. "Humor me. I'm pregnant. I get strange cravings, and I can't tell from one day to the next what they will be for."

Danny just smiled and signaled for the waiter. He was getting pretty familiar with cravings. In his case, though, they were not for food.

He enjoyed the easy camaraderie that had begun to develop between them almost as much as he loved the special moments, the lovemaking. Now, if he could just figure out how to propose to her and be certain that Ally would accept, he could die happy.

Then he remembered his pending assignment to Tamahlyastan and amended himself. Of course he hoped it wouldn't come to that. At least not for another fifty or sixty years.

DARKNESS HAD FALLEN by the time they finished at O'Malley's, but the evening air was still balmy, thanks to the lingering Indian summer.

Ally paused outside the restaurant and let the warm breeze caress her cheek. "What a wonderful night for a stroll in the park," she said.

Danny reached around her, fitting his hand into the curve of her waist. "Yeah, it is nice," he said, and lifted his face to the breeze. "Too bad we have to go see the captain." With gentle pressure to Ally's waist, he steered her toward the waiting car.

She couldn't help thinking that this was one of those postcard moments that made a courtship beautiful. Of course, this wasn't an ordinary courtship. After all, the courting had been done long ago.

Now they were just trying to work out the details for the rest of their lives. And what happened in the next few days would determine their future. If Danny proposed again, she would accept—after making some concessions, she supposed—and they'd have their happily-ever-after.

If not, they would have to figure out how to keep Danny in the baby's life, but not necessarily in hers. That was a future she did not want.

Though Ally was happy that Danny had decided to come out of his cave to be with her tonight, she still didn't have a real feel for his current mindset. Yes, he'd proposed to her. Several days ago and on the spur of the moment. Had he really meant it?

Yes, he'd suggested that he might propose again, but now that she'd decided that she would accept him, he hadn't broached the subject. How was she going to get him to do it so she could say yes, while making him believe that it was *his* idea?

They stopped at a light and Ally glanced over at Danny, illuminated by the glow. In the red glare, Danny looked like the fierce warrior he was trained to be, yet he had shown her another side of him as he'd opened up to the idea of their baby and the prospect of being a father.

Ally had loved Danny as he was almost three years ago, but now that they'd both matured, so had her love.

As they drove through the dark streets toward Roger Haddad's off-base neighborhood, Ally knew one thing for sure. She would accept any proposal from Danny in an instant, with no reservations, if he'd just ask.

DANNY COULDN'T HELP grinning at Ally seated cross-legged on Haddad's garage floor surrounded by the litter of squirming puppies just like a kid. No, she looked just like their kid would look some fifteen years or so from now.

Who wouldn't be in love with that beautiful woman sitting in front of him?

Ally glanced up at him, two wriggling puppies in her arms. "I can't decide which, Danny. They're both so adorable," she said as one pup licked at her face while the other one decided to make a snack of her long, jet-black hair. "You've got to help me."

Danny hunkered down beside her and took the

hair chewer out of her hands. "Do you really want this one? You'd have to keep your hair pinned up all the time, and that would be a damn shame."

Ally beamed at his comment. "Yes, but I'd have to constantly be fixing my makeup with this one," Ally pointed out as she held the face licker away from her.

"Why do you bother with makeup anyway, Ally? You always look beautiful to me."

Ally glowed with pleasure from the compliment, and Danny caught Amy Haddad giving her husband a knowing nudge. He guessed his feelings for Ally, and hers for him, weren't as carefully hidden as he'd thought, but at this late date, he no longer cared.

He had just a few more days to figure out what to do. Then he had to make it happen.

Seeing Ally, sitting happily on the floor amid the puppies, he couldn't help musing that maybe the whole mess just might work out after all.

If it didn't, it wouldn't be for lack of trying on his part.

In the middle of all this, Ally seemed oblivious to his deep thinking, but Danny didn't really mind. What had to be said between them was best said in private.

Ally glanced up, her chin damp from wet puppy kisses, and grinned like a kid. "I guess it's gonna be Sweetie-Pie here," she announced.

Danny took the pup out of her hands and turned it over. Correction—turned *him* over. "Now wait just a minute, Allison Carter. You will not ruin a perfectly good guy dog with a stupid name like Sweetie-Pie."

Making a face at him, Ally took the puppy back. "He's my Sweetie-Pie, and I can call him anything I want." She gazed at the pup. "Can't I, Sweetie-Pie?"

If Ally would promise to be his Sweetie-Pie, Danny thought, he wouldn't give a damn what she called him, either.

Sweetie-Pie took that moment to sprinkle her lap, and Danny had to laugh. "I guess Water Boy had other ideas."

Ally cuddled the puppy. "It's okay, little guy. I forgive you this time, and the right name will come to us sooner or later. I love you anyway," she whispered.

He closed his hand over Ally's and helped her and the puppy up. Then he turned to the Haddads. "Sweetie-Pie here is the one."

Amy Haddad smiled. "Most people don't realize that they can't name puppies—puppies name themselves." She smiled at Ally. "I think you made a good choice."

Ally beamed. "I do, too."

She was pretty sure Danny wasn't referring to the dog.

"I guess we'll have to stop at the pet store for supplies on the way home."

Danny liked the way she said "home," even if it really wasn't his. Yet. "That we can do," he said, then he looked Ally square in the eyes. "Then we'll discuss names."

He was pretty sure she understood they weren't talking about the puppy's.

ALLY WAS AFRAID they wouldn't make it to the pet shop on time. Puppy cradled in her arms, she and Danny dashed into the store just moments before it closed. After throwing themselves on the mercy of the tired manager, and with the help of the store clerk, they got what they needed.

"Thank you so much for taking the time with us," Ally said as one of the staff rang up all her purchases. Danny blanched at the total, but Ally presented her debit card without a moment's hesitation. If Danny didn't say anything, she wouldn't, either.

Sometimes, knowing when to keep your mouth shut was the best way to get along, she had recently concluded. She understood that if she was going to make a relationship with Danny work, she would have to concede on some issues. Danny would have to compromise, as well.

"Yeah," Danny added. "We knew better than to try to get all this so late, but we just couldn't take this little guy home without the best of everything."

The manager, a tired-looking woman of middle age, smiled. "It makes my day to help such a happy little family," she said.

Danny didn't correct her, and Ally simply smiled. *From your lips to God's ears,* she couldn't help thinking.

She turned to Danny. "Well, let's get our 'son' home and tucked in," she said. "We've all had a long day."

"Got that in one," he agreed. Then, to the obvious relief of the store personnel, he gathered up their purchases and led the way outside.

DANNY PACED in the living room, waiting for Ally to tuck the little fellow into his crate in her bedroom. He was gonna do it, he told himself. Tonight he was going to make sure that Ally knew how he felt. He was almost certain that if he asked her to marry him, this time she would accept.

Now, if they could just get on with it.

He wondered whether he should have bought a ring, but he hadn't been certain until tonight when the moment would be right. Should he get down on one knee the way they did in the movies? He wanted to do it properly, but he wasn't a one-knee kind of guy. And if he had to have a ring, he'd have to put his proposal off till another day.

"No," he told himself firmly. "Tonight's the night."

"Did you say something, Danny?"

When had Ally come into the room? He pivoted to face her. Damn, she was beautiful. She'd kicked off her shoes and slipped into some sort of flowing robe-type thing in that dark pink color she'd once told him was fuchsia. Whatever color it was, she looked hot in it. She couldn't have prepared for this unexpected moment better if he'd told her what to wear.

"Are you sure that crate isn't too big for the little

guy?" he asked, to divert Ally's attention from what she might have heard him muttering.

"Positive," Ally said, a little confused at his question.

Had she expected him to ask something else?

"He needs room to move around if he's going to be in there all day when I'm not at home," Ally continued. "And he will grow."

"Yeah, they do that, don't they." Danny wasn't entirely sure whether he was talking about the dog or their baby. He was still new to both: puppy ownership and fatherhood.

But, he reminded himself, he'd best get used to the ideas. He'd just signed on to be responsible for a puppy and he was about to do the same for Ally and their baby.

"Whew," he whistled, stepping closer. "You're more gorgeous every time I see you."

Ally beamed with pleasure. "Thank you," she said, staring up at him, her dark, dark eyes wide with anticipation.

Could she be as ready for this as he was?

"We fat pregnant ladies need all the reassurance we can get, even if it isn't true."

"It is true, Ally. Every word of it," Danny whispered, his voice husky with emotion. He took Ally's hands and drew her to him, then bent to her, touching her forehead with his. He loved this kind of closeness.

"Ally, you are the most beautiful woman I have ever known. You're all I ever wanted. I don't care how much weight you gain. It's natural."

"Well, I hope it doesn't come to that," Ally said with a chuckle.

"You know what I mean," Danny said. "Here," he went on. "Let's sit down." He inclined his head toward the sofa, then cleared his throat. "I have something important to ask you."

Ally's eyes grew even wider. "Yes?" she said, sinking slowly and gracefully to the cushions.

Boy, this was hard, Danny thought. Why couldn't he just blurt out the proposal and get it over with? No, he told himself. He had to do this perfectly. This was way too important.

The rest of his life hinged on the next few moments. He let go of Ally's hands only long enough to wipe his on his pantlegs. "Ally?" he said, then he shook his head and cleared his throat again.

"Yes, Danny?" she prompted.

Did she know what he was getting at? Of course she did. She had to. Then why the hell didn't she help him out here. He started again. "Ally, I want you to be my wife," he finally managed to say.

Ally nodded, but she seemed to be waiting for more. She glanced downward.

Danny touched her chin and tipped her face upward. He kissed her on lips that trembled with emotion. The sweetness, the tenderness of response overwhelmed him. "Will you do me the honor of becoming Mrs. Allison Murphey?"

Her eyes filled with tears, and Ally blinked them away. She nodded again—frantically. "Yes, yes, yes," she said. "I want so much to be your wife."

Danny threw his arms around her and squeezed her to him. "Thank you so much. I intend to be the best father to our child," he said, wanting her to know for certain that he loved the baby, too.

"I know you do, Danny," Ally said softly.

He clasped his hands excitedly. "What do we do next? We have to get started," he announced. "We have to make plans!" Now that she'd said yes, he didn't want anything to get in the way of their beginning the rest of their lives.

"Hey, hold on there, Sergeant," Ally said, raising up one small hand like a traffic cop. "We have plenty of time."

"No, we don't. We have only a few months till the baby comes. And I'll be leaving here Saturday morning to go back to Hurlburt. And not long after that, I'll be taking off for Tamahlyastan." Now that he'd done it, Danny didn't want to fool around with petty things like details. He wanted to get on with the program.

"We have to get a marriage license. We have to find a preacher."

"Yes, there is that," Ally said. "And I do want to marry you—the sooner the better. But we have some technicalities to settle."

Danny shook his head vehemently. "No, no. All I need is to give you my name. Give my child my name."

Ally held her hand up again. "That name thing is one of those details we have to talk about. I love you more than life itself, and I want to be your wife." She paused as if trying to figure out what to say next, then she took a deep breath and charged on. "Would you mind very much if I kept my family name?"

He felt as though she'd detonated an eighty-megaton atom bomb. "What?"

"For business purposes," Ally said calmly. "I need to continue to use Carter. You don't mind, do you?"

Danny pushed himself to his feet and glared down at her. He could not believe she would even think of asking that after all they'd been through. What should he say? How should he react? He had not anticipated anything like this! Not even on a bad day.

He opened his mouth to speak, but then snapped it shut to keep from saying the wrong thing. He turned toward the door. He had to get out of there. He had to think.

"Danny? What's wrong?"

"What's wrong?" he bellowed. "I'll tell you what's wrong. I just offered my life to you, and you... you...just—"

"I accepted," Ally said, looking as if she had no idea what he was getting at, acting as if he'd hurt her feelings.

Her feelings? he thought indignantly. What about his?

"No, you didn't. Here I was, ready to lay my life on the line for you. Make an honorable woman out of you. Give your baby my name. And you throw my proposal back at me like it means nothing to you?" he shouted.

Ally shrank from him for a moment, but then rose

to face him. "*My* baby?" She sounded incredulous. "I'm not sure I want to marry you after all, Danny Murphey. I agreed to be your wife. That ought to be enough."

"Well, it isn't," Danny fired back. "I'm an old-fashioned kind of guy. I want everyone to know that you're mine. I offered you my name. I offered you everything I have."

Ally drew herself up to her full five feet. "Don't do me any favors, Murphey. I don't need you to take care of me. I am not a prize breeding cow to be branded so that everyone who sees *me* knows who owns me. I am perfectly capable of taking care of myself. *And* your baby. Until you figure that out, I'll just continue to do exactly that." She glared at him.

Danny had no quick retort, nothing he could say.

He wanted to strangle her.

He wanted to kiss her.

He wanted to go back in time and start again. But there wouldn't be any do-overs tonight.

Danny strode to the door, yanked it open and rushed outside. He slammed it so hard behind him that the frame rattled.

When the cool night air hit him, Danny stopped. What the hell had just happened? He had been in the middle of the best moment of his life and then everything had disintegrated.

He turned and raised his fist to knock on the door, but reconsidered. He needed to think. Maybe Ally needed to think just as much as he did.

He damn sure didn't need to stay here and make the situation worse. If it could get any worse.

He hurried to the rental car and let himself inside. Even then, he couldn't make himself drive away.

What was he doing just sitting there? Did he hope that Ally might come running out after him, begging for forgiveness?

He waited for what seemed an eternity, but when the door didn't open, Danny turned the key in the ignition and pulled slowly out of the driveway.

Chapter Thirteen

Ally sank limply onto the couch and stared at the door that Danny had just slammed so violently that the noise still echoed deep in her soul. Surely Danny would realize what she'd been trying to tell him. Surely he would understand that she wasn't rejecting him and come back.

He had to.

"Everything was so perfect," she wailed. "Why did I have to pick tonight to bring that stupid issue up? Why did I have to open my big mouth?"

If she didn't love Danny so much, she'd almost think she had been trying to drive him away.

When Ally didn't hear Danny's car start and the irrevocable sound of him driving away from her, she dared to hope. The silence surrounded her as she counted the minutes, it seemed to cling to her, to suffocate her, as she waited for some sign.

Just as she decided that she would have to make the first move and pushed herself to her feet, starting toward the door to bring him back, to beg him if she had to, she heard it.

The engine started up.

Ally rushed to the door and tried to open it, but the lock, slammed with such violence, had accidentally engaged. She fumbled with the latch, her fingers clumsy and uncooperative. Danny *had* to return. She needed to apologize, to ask his forgiveness.

Finally, the recalcitrant mechanism gave way.

"Danny, Danny, come back!" she called frantically as she flung open the door.

It was too late.

She stood in the doorway and stared at the twin red taillights, which looked like the angry eyes of a retreating demon, taunting her as they grew smaller and dimmer in the distance.

Ally watched until the lights disappeared around the corner, then she slowly turned.

On boneless legs she walked back inside. With trembling hands, she locked the door behind her.

What had she just done?

Like a robot, she trudged to her bedroom.

The puppy must have heard the commotion, because Ally heard his frightened whimpering as she stepped into the room. She hurried to his crate, but she didn't see him in it. At last, she found him cowering in a corner.

Tamping down her own anguish, Ally crouched and quietly called the puppy to her. "Come here, Sweetie-Pie," she crooned, trying very hard to push her heartbreak out of her voice. "I won't hurt you. It's all right," she coaxed.

The puppy crept toward her, and when he was

within reach, Ally scooped him up into her arms and held him gently to her breast. His tiny heart seemed to race a hundred miles an hour as she held him to her. "I'm so sorry, Sweetie-Pie," she whispered, attempting to soothe him. "I didn't mean to drive Daddy away."

The puppy grew calmer, and as he did, so did she. Ally didn't know why she thought everything would turn out in the end, but she had to hope it would.

Danny was an intelligent man, even if he was often far too hotheaded. Surely, when he took some time to think about what she'd really said to him, he'd realize that she hadn't completely rejected his name and, therefore him.

He had to.

She wanted so much to be Mrs. Murphey that it hurt. "Now I just have to figure out how to make sure that he knows it." Ally gazed at the tiny brown creature huddled in her arms. "It'll be all right, little one. It will all work out."

The baby kicked her soundly, and Ally wasn't sure whether it was in agreement with her statement or a way of showing an objection to what her stupid mother had done. Whatever the reason, Ally felt she deserved it.

"You're absolutely right, baby girl. I feel like kicking myself, too," she murmured.

"I promise you, little Danielle," she went on as she settled the puppy back into his crate. "You will grow up with a daddy who loves you. And loves me, too," she added without quite as much conviction.

"Danielle Murphey," she repeated, savoring the feel of the name on her tongue, listening to the sound. She didn't know why the name had come to her with such certainty now, but it seemed right.

She got up and placed her hand over her stomach. "You will grow up with a traditional, happy family—mommy, daddy, puppy and all."

The baby kicked her as if to second that emotion.

THOUGH DANNY TRIED to temper his anger on the drive back to the Q, the frustration finally got to him. Seeing an open slot near the front door, he gunned the engine and screeched in, then he slammed on the brakes. His first thought had been to go somewhere and to lay on a drunk, but good sense won over. After all, he still had three days of this class to get through.

He was going into a combat zone and his life might depend on it.

The rest of his life might also hang on what he said and did with Ally, he realized.

He switched off the headlights and sat for a moment in the darkness, the street lamp on the far side of the lot the only illumination. He had to get a handle on this thing. On differences he and Ally had.

And what they had in common.

Maybe if he stayed away from her for a couple of days he'd be more objective.

That was it, he decided. He would keep Ally out of his line of sight until he'd had a chance to thoroughly think through all their options.

He loved that exasperating, aggravating…beautiful woman with every ounce of his being. And if it meant skulking around in corridors and making himself scarce until he could figure her out, then so be it.

He might leave this place alone, but it would not be because he'd driven Ally from his life.

He'd leave because his job forced him to.

Sometimes, honor and duty were a crock.

ALLY WOULDN'T GO OUT of her way to avoid Danny, but she wouldn't hide, either.

As it happened, she didn't have to. Danny seemed to be ducking behind furniture every time she appeared. She knew he needed time to think, but she also knew that his time was limited.

If he didn't come to his senses in the next two days, it would be too late.

Might be too late, she amended, ever hopeful.

She wished he would at least speak to her. Then she'd stand a chance of getting a feel for his state of mind. She stepped out of her office and into the hall on one of her frequent trips to the bathroom and walked right into him.

"Excuse me—" Danny stopped. "Oh, Ally," he said carefully.

At least he hadn't called her Ms. Carter, Ally thought, hoping that Danny's failure to address her formally was an encouraging sign.

"I'm sorry," she said. "My fault." She wanted him to understand what she was talking about. Ally knew that the corridor of Building 4527 was not the right

place to work things out, but she had to try to communicate her willingness to do so. "I should have
been watching where I was going," she added.

"Yeah, you should have," Danny replied, and they
both understood that he wasn't referring to where she
was going in this hallway.

"I want to compromise," Ally said.

"You do that, Ally," Danny said, then pivoted and
strode down the hall in the opposite direction. "I'll do
the same," he called, looking back over his shoulder.

Ally wanted to follow him, to catch him by the
sleeve of the battle-dress uniform and make him stay
and talk to her. Danny shoved open the heavy exterior door, letting in a shaft of light that made her blink
because of its brilliance. Ally knew she had to let him
go. He still had to get his thoughts together about this.

About them.

That he hadn't rejected her outright this morning
was encouraging, even though it wasn't nearly enough.

Ally watched Danny withdraw his scarlet beret
from his uniform pocket and jam it onto his head. He
was adjusting it to the precise, regulation-mandated
angle as the door swung shut between them.

That was the picture of Danny she'd always carried in her mind's eye, the one she'd always carry
with her. She didn't want this week to be the last time
she would see him for real.

Remembering her original purpose for being in
the hall, Ally hurried on. It wasn't much progress, but
she did feel as though she and Danny had made a
little.

She just hoped it wasn't too little, too late.

And she sure wished that Kathie Palmore were around to talk it over with. There were times when a woman just needed a sympathetic ear.

But it wasn't a substitute for a strong shoulder.

THE SUN WAS BARELY UP when Danny and Jake hurried out for their daily exercise. Today was the last day of class, and weather that had been balmy all week had begun to change. The sky, just beginning to lighten, was thick with clouds and the air heavy with the threat of rain. Danny didn't care. If it rained, so what? He'd just cool down that much quicker.

He'd used his daily run for the past few days as time to think, really think, and to clear his head for the day before him. If the truth be told, he wanted a way to work off his frustrations. His feet operating on automatic, his thoughts churned as he and Jake trotted from the Q to the base exercise field. As they approached the running track, Danny increased his pace, feeling his feet pound against the pavement, feeling his anger leave him and some sort of calm come to him.

Soon he'd left Jake Magnussen far behind.

"Hey, man," Jake shouted after him. "Lighten up. It's only PT. It isn't supposed to be a freakin' competition."

At first, when Danny thought back to the other night, all he remembered was the emotional slap in the face he'd experienced when Ally had said she didn't want to take his name. All he could feel was anger.

But time did strange things.

Danny slowed, but not because of Jake. He slowed because he'd finally started to understand some of what had happened.

The more he thought about it, time or common sense or something else made him remember exactly what Ally had said that night, not what he'd thought he'd heard. She'd said "for professional reasons."

Not for her personal life. *Their* personal life. At least, that was what Danny wanted to believe she meant. She didn't say that she didn't want that.

Funny, at one time he would have gone ballistic at the idea of her having any kind of professional life. Livid at the notion that she might believe he couldn't provide for her. But some of the things she'd pointed out to him had finally sunk in.

Why shouldn't she work if it made her happy? Why couldn't they have a marriage where they shared everything? Including providing for their child.

Maybe if his own parents had done that, his father would be around to see his next grandchild. Danny's first child.

He checked his watch and slowed his pace. He'd been running long enough; it was time to get back to the Q and shower before class.

Jake loped up behind him, his face red and dripping with sweat. "Hey, man, so you've been majorly funked up the past couple of days. You don't have to take it out on me."

Jake was right. "Didn't mean to," Danny grumbled.

"You say something?" Jake slowed and fell into step with him.

Danny looked up. "What? I was thinking. I didn't mean to put it on you," he said. And he shouldn't have taken it out on Ally, either.

"Well, if this is what being in love means, then I don't want anything to do with it," Jake said, pulling his sweat-soaked shirt up over his head and blotting his face with it. "Give me a no-strings roll in the hay anytime."

There had been a period when Danny might have agreed with the man, but circumstances had changed. Hell, *he* had changed. He was in love. He'd tried to fall out of it, and it hadn't happened.

"Well, I am in love," Danny finally said, wondering how the hell Jake knew. "And it is right for me." Damn, he wasn't sure he'd ever said that before, he just realized. He wasn't even sure he'd ever said it to Ally. Not in so many words, anyway.

Maybe that was what he had to do. And why hadn't he done it before?

One thing was sure, he vowed to himself as he and Jake silently trudged back to the Q to shower up before class. "I'm gonna do it," he muttered, not caring whether Jake heard it or not.

He would not leave this place without making Ally and their child his.

For real and for always.

ALLY WOKE UP LATE, feeling sluggish and tired. She hadn't slept very well. For the past few nights, she'd had to get up several times to take the puppy out.

And of course, this forced separation from Danny wasn't exactly what she wanted, either. But until Danny came out of his cave, she would leave him alone.

Yawning, she sat up in bed. If this was what it was like to carry a child, she was finally beginning to understand what Danny had meant when he'd suggested that working and having a baby would not be quite the effortless, natural process she'd expected.

She hadn't imagined how tired she would be after being awakened twice last night, even if only for a few minutes each time. She hadn't realized how important it would be to sleep the entire night.

Still, she told herself as she stumbled toward her reviving morning shower, "Babies sleep through the night eventually. Surely I can take leave long enough to get past that part."

She had to. Even if she and Danny did come to terms and planned to make a life together. She wrapped a towel around her hair and stepped into the shower.

Legally married or not and on the same wavelength about their roles in life or not, because of Danny's assignment in Tamahlyastan, she would not have him around to help her through.

That was something she would really have to think about. Ally guessed she would need to talk to Kathie about it. After all, the colonel had been through it three times. And Ally remembered Kathie's husband hadn't been around for one of them.

Meanwhile, she had to get ready for work. She dressed, fed the puppy, took him outside, then settled him into the crate. Yep, if this was a dress rehearsal for parenthood, she would need a lot more practice, Ally thought as she popped a couple of pieces of wheat toast into the toaster, then peeled the plastic wrap off a slice of cheese while the bread toasted.

Dropping an apple into her purse for later, Ally waited for the bread to come up. When it did, she slipped the cheese between the two slices, gathered up her belongings and headed out the door.

Yes, maybe Danny hadn't really been talking about popcorn when he'd told her she needed a dog. Maybe she just needed the puppy for a reality check.

Sometimes, it was best to learn something the hard way, she grudgingly admitted. While she might possess quite a bit of book knowledge about life, she hadn't had that many opportunities to test out the practical applications.

Whatever his reasons for suggesting a dog, she would thank Danny Murphey for doing it.

She needed a reason to talk to him, anyway.

"WE'RE GOING to O'Malley's for lunch," Lieutenant Abernathy announced once Mr. Saloam dismissed class. "You in?"

Danny grinned. The lieutenant had come a long way since that first day in class. He had learned that she would be attached to his unit in Tamahlyastan, and he was almost looking forward to serving with her. "Wish I could, Lieutenant, but I've got an important errand to take care of. I guess I'll just grab a burger."

"Too bad," the lieutenant said. "Does it have anything to do with one female instructor who shall, for purposes of this discussion, remain nameless?"

Holding a thumb up, Danny answered, "I'll never tell."

He turned, to find himself face-to-face with the instructor in question. "Ally?"

"In the flesh," she said. "I do work here. Why should you be surprised to run into me?"

Danny opened his mouth to explain, then snapped it shut. No sense spoiling the surprise. "It doesn't matter. I just wasn't expecting to see you now."

"Obviously," Ally said dryly. "You really should watch where you're going. Somebody could get hurt." As if to emphasize her statement, she placed her hand protectively over her stomach.

If she only knew how much that turned him on, Danny thought, she wouldn't do it so often. Then again, maybe she did know and was doing it on purpose. He smiled. No, it wasn't a sexual turn-on, but a turn-on, anyway. Maybe the gesture always reminded him of the most important person in the middle of this stupid mess. The one person he hadn't really been thinking about when he'd let his pride get in the way.

"Sorry, I was in a hurry."

Ally glanced back toward the lieutenant, her dark eyes clouding. "Got a hot date?"

"What?" Danny wanted to say he only had eyes for her, but he didn't want to play his hand quite so soon. "Oh, her? Abernathy wanted everybody to go to O'Malley's for a last-day-of-class lunch. Some of the guys are leaving right after class this afternoon."

"I guess that means you won't want to come over to my house for lunch today," she said, sounding disappointed.

"I'm not going with them," Danny said, reaching into his pocket for his keys. "I've got something else to do." He really had to get on with it, and Ally was holding him up. He started toward the door, then stopped. "Why are you going home? Don't you usually eat here?"

"I have to check on Sweetie-Pie. Need to let him out of his crate. He's only a little guy. He can't stay by himself all day."

"Sort of like having a baby, huh?" Danny said, trying not to demonstrate his distraction.

"Why didn't you say that when we went to pick him up?"

"Would you have listened?"

Time was wasting, Danny kept thinking, eyeing the door and still hoping for a quick getaway. What he had to do really wouldn't wait.

Ally laughed. "Probably not. And you made your point, even if you didn't mean to. Having a puppy is pretty much like having a newborn, isn't it."

"Got that in one," Danny said, even if he hadn't intended to make that particular point.

"Anyhow, I've got to go home and let him out before he has an accident." She turned. "I was hoping we'd be able to talk before you left."

"Me, too," Danny said huskily. "Can I take you to dinner tonight?"

Ally smiled brightly enough to burn the clouds out of the sky. "With pleasure. Of course, we'll have to go home and attend to Sweetie-Pie first. Walk me to the car?"

"All right, then," Danny said, offering his arm. "I'll meet you after work, and we'll take care of Bruiser. You are going to have to give him a guy name, you know," he reminded her again. "He's gonna get a complex."

"We'll see," Ally said as he pushed open the heavy exterior door. "I suppose we can discuss names later."

They parted smiling, and headed to their respective cars, parked on opposite ends of the lot. Danny hustled through the autumn drizzle, his plans whirling in his head. Tonight was going to be perfect. He wouldn't let anything spoil it.

He watched as Ally slipped into her own little automobile. Then, once she was out of sight, he inserted his key into the ignition, started the engine and backed out of the slot. He snatched a quick look at his watch.

He had exactly fifty-three minutes at his disposal.

"BYE, LITTLE SWEETIE-PIE," Ally called softly as she latched the puppy securely into his crate. He whimpered in response. Ally wanted so much to pick him up and hug him one more time, but she'd already stayed too long, happy to accept yet another round of puppy kisses.

She hurried out of the house and into her car, barely noticing the occasional drops of rain as another shower began. She had her umbrella. What was a little rain when she was so happy?

There'd been good news in the mailbox when Ally had checked. She'd finally gotten a letter from a long-lost aunt, or second cousin, or something— she wasn't really certain what the relationship was. It didn't really matter because this woman was one of the only blood relatives she had in the world.

To know that someone out there was connected to her by ties of blood that couldn't be severed was so reassuring. Ally patted her tummy. Of course she wouldn't be alone once Danielle was born, but she liked the idea of having family.

Ally hummed contentedly as she backed her car out of her driveway and drove to the base. She had always wondered what unconditional love would feel like, and the past few days with Sweetie-Pie, or Bruiser, or Ralph, or whatever they'd end up naming him, had shown her how it could be. Realizing that she'd included Danny's input in the naming of the puppy, she smiled. She was already thinking about the two of them as a unit.

As she cruised down the road toward the base, she rubbed at her face. Sweetie-Pie had nearly licked her senseless when she'd let him in after his potty break, and she probably should have checked her makeup. Thinking of his puppy kisses, she glanced into the mirror. In spite of the devastation to her makeup, she smiled again.

Ally had barely made it out onto the main road when the cloudburst began in earnest, but even the sudden onset of rain couldn't dampen her spirits.

Tonight, she and Danny would finally come to an agreement. Tonight, she and Danny would start to plan the rest of their lives.

She would do whatever he wanted, just as long as she could be his wife. She would stay home, barefoot and pregnant, to play a permanent part in Danny's life—a prospect that had begun to seem very inviting after her trial run at motherhood with the puppy.

Even a mud hut in the mountains of Tamahlyastan would be home if Danny lived there with her. Ally had learned so much in the years she and Danny had been apart, in the months since she'd discovered she was carrying his child, and the days since he'd come to town and found out she was carrying his child.

Ally didn't care that the sky was gray and stormy this afternoon. Tonight would be special.

Her mind was so focused on the evening ahead that she didn't see the delivery truck that hadn't yielded the right of way as he merged onto the four-lane highway.

"Oh, my God," she gasped, as she jammed her foot on the brake pedal. The brakes locked and the car slid sideways on the wet and slippery road.

Then she didn't see anything else.

Chapter Fourteen

Danny found it hard to keep his mind on Captain Haddad's presentation that afternoon. He was too focused on what was going to happen tonight. Make that what he *wanted* to happen.

They had taken their final test yesterday afternoon and today was mainly a formality. They would receive certificates of completion and rehash what they'd learned. A lot of the guys were heading out this afternoon, so it didn't make sense to have the exam this late. And it was a damn good thing for Danny. Considering his present state of mind, he would have failed it for sure.

Tonight would be the first day of the rest of his life. Or so he hoped. As much as he'd thought about it, he couldn't think of a reason that Ally wouldn't accept his proposal this time.

Finally, Captain Haddad dismissed the class. An hour early. Hoo-ah! Danny could have turned back flips, but instead, he gathered up the folder containing his certificate and other paperwork and filed out of the room with the rest of the class.

After all, he wasn't positive he'd get the girl. Yet. He still had to ask her and she still had to accept. He'd save the celebrations for later.

He had agreed to meet Ally at her house after class, but since he was finished early and she was most likely still working in her office, he decided to take a chance. He stepped into the reception area that fronted the warren of instructors' offices. The receptionist wasn't there. However, in typical government-issue fashion, there was a placard on Ally's door, so he knew exactly which one was hers.

The door was ajar, but out of politeness, he knocked first. Then he stepped inside.

A blond woman, obviously not Ally, was standing at the desk, one hand resting on a stack of papers. He thought she was Betty, the secretary, but her back was to him. She appeared to be staring into space. Danny rapped again. Obviously startled, the secretary spun around.

"Oh, you surprised me," the woman said.

Yes, she was the secretary he'd met a week or so ago. Betty Rodkey, he thought. Only then did Danny notice that Betty's eyes were red and her normally pretty face was streaked with tears.

"Are you lost?" she asked.

"No," he said, regretting his intrusion into the woman's private moment.

"I was looking for A— I mean Ms. Carter," he amended.

Betty began to say something, but instead gulped

in air, sort of like a grounded guppy. Then her face crumpled and she began to sob.

"I'm sorry," Danny said. "Maybe I should leave and come back later."

"No," Betty answered sharply. "You don't know, do you?"

"No-o-o," Danny said slowly, wondering what the hell was going on here. "What don't I know?"

"You are Danny Murphey? Ally's friend?"

"Yes, I'm Murphey."

"I was just going through her desk trying to find something with your VAQ address, or a phone number, or something so I could reach you."

"Okay, you got me," he said bluntly. "What do you want me for?"

Danny tried to swallow a lump in his throat the size of a hand grenade. Why was Ally sending her secretary to give him a message? Surely this wasn't another big kiss-off....

"Ally's been in an accident," Betty said in a rush, as if she was trying to get the information out before starting to lose it again.

Danny felt as though the hand grenade had gone off in his chest, and he gasped from the shock. "What happened?" he asked thickly.

"A truck ran a red light, I believe. Ally swerved to avoid it, but she skidded into a cement barricade."

"Is she…?" Danny couldn't, wouldn't, let himself complete the question.

"She's going to be all right," the secretary said,

though Danny didn't think she looked all that positive.

"What hospital?" He had to get to Ally. Had to be there to help her.

The secretary told him, and he sprinted into the hall before she had a chance to finish her sentence, much less give him the address. He damn sure didn't have precious minutes to waste listening to unnecessary directions.

Betty had named the main hospital downtown, and Danny knew right where that was. He'd seen it a couple of times as he'd driven through town.

The woman he loved was there. He had to get to her. He had to be there. He had to make sure himself that she was all right.

A HARRIED NURSE was bustling around the room fiddling with machines and jotting notes on a chart when Ally woke up. She was attached to a fetal monitor, her doctor had told her earlier, but she had no idea what the various lines and squiggles on the display and the beeps it made really meant.

The nurse turned to adjust the IV drip, and Ally tried to speak, but her throat and tongue were dry.

"Oh, you're awake," the woman said.

Again, Ally tried to speak, but her parched throat wouldn't work.

"Let me get you some water," the nurse said. "I'll be right back, then we can talk."

Ally struggled to push herself upright, but she

was tethered to so many wires and tubes that she was, for all practical purposes, pinned to the mattress.

She couldn't even manage to reach one hand around to touch her stomach. She would feel so much better, so reassured, if Danielle would just give her one big thump.

Apparently, Danielle wasn't cooperating. Or… No. Ally shook her head. She could not bring herself even to contemplate the alternative.

Dr. Schmale, her obstetrician, came in, and Ally again tried to voice her concerns.

"It's all right, Allison. You're going to be just fine."

Ally wanted to scream. Dammit all. Didn't the doctor understand that she didn't care about herself. She shook her head violently and attempted to mouth her question. She finally managed to whisper the one word most important to her.

"Baby," she rasped.

Dr. Schmale glanced at her chart at the foot of the bed. "There's a small problem." Then she sat down on the chair at bedside and explained.

How DANNY got to the hospital without being caught breaking any traffic laws was a miracle. That he got there and found a spot in the car park immediately adjacent to the front door was even better.

Danny slammed on the brakes, cut the engine and ejected himself as if making egress from a plane at twenty thousand feet rather than hitting terra firma from ground level. Snatching his red beret from his head, he dashed through the automatic doors and up to the information desk.

"Allison Carter," he gasped. "She was in an automobile accident earlier today. Where is she?"

The woman turned and typed something—the name, Danny assumed—into the computer. He waited what seemed like an eternity for the computer to cough up the secret. "Can't you hurry it up?"

"It's working as fast as it can," the woman said, without bothering to look up at him. "Ah," she said. "Here it comes."

Danny didn't need the woman's stalling tactics. He wanted to snatch her from behind her glass partition and shake her. "Tell me," he demanded. "Where?"

The woman did, and instructed him to follow a green line on the floor.

He did as she told him, only to be stopped short at the closed elevator doors. He pressed the Up button, then mashed it again when the doors didn't open. Still, no elevator came to answer his bidding. He was about to find the stairs when the elevator finally came and discharged its load of people.

Silently issuing a prayer, he stepped on board and pressed the floor number. *God, let her be all right,* he prayed silently. *God, let her be all right,* he repeated as the elevator slowly carried him upward.

He found the nurses' station and, planning only to pause long enough to ask for directions, barked out his question. "Allison Carter's room?"

"I'm sorry, Mr.—" The nurse on guard stopped to read his name tag. "Sergeant Murphey, you can't go in there right now. The doctor is with her."

What the hell is all this? Danny's heart was racing and his breath short from the adrenaline rush he'd been operating on since he'd gotten the word from Ally's secretary.

What were they not telling him? "Can you tell me about her condition? The baby's?"

The woman reluctantly shook her head. "I'm sorry, I don't know. Are you a relative?"

"No. Not yet, anyway," Danny said, hoping he'd still get the chance to change that. "I was going to propose tonight." As an afterthought, he added, "I'm the baby's father."

The nurse smiled. "I'm sure the doctor will be out in a minute. I appreciate that it's hard not knowing exactly what's going on," she said sympathetically. "You can sit in the waiting area over there, and I'll call you the minute the doctor comes out."

Danny did as he was told. He was used to being told what to do, following orders. Too bad somebody couldn't tell him how to behave and what to feel at this moment, because he sure didn't know.

If anything serious had happened to Ally, to the baby, he had no idea what he would do.

Damn, he felt helpless.

He tried to sit in the deserted waiting area, but he was too edgy. Too distracted to read months-old issues of tattered news magazines. He paced back and forth from the hallway door to the window that looked out onto the wet car park. Just like the expectant father he was.

Or was he?

He couldn't help thinking that none of this would have happened if he and Ally had never broken up in the first place. If he'd just been smart enough to keep his mouth shut.

"Sergeant Murphey?"

Danny pivoted toward a sweet-faced woman with light brown hair, who was standing in the doorway to the waiting room. She was dressed in a white lab coat that covered a blue business suit. He didn't know why he noticed—maybe it was simply a tactic to keep himself from worrying. Whatever she was wearing, she was obviously the doctor.

"You're Ally's physician?"

The woman gave him a reassuring smile. "Yes, I'm Debra Schmale." She offered her hand, and Danny accepted it. "Your fiancée is going to be fine. You can go in now. I'm sure she'll be happy to see you."

Relief rushed through him. Still, the doctor hadn't said anything about…"The baby?" Danny finally made himself ask.

"Why don't you go be with Ally. She's needs you more than you need to talk to me. She's in the third room on the left." Smiling tiredly, the doctor effectively dismissed him.

Danny slowly walked down the hall to Ally's room, wondering what he would find when he reached it. He had not received a straight answer from anyone about the baby. *Was* there still a baby?

How cruel of them to keep him in the dark! Or did they think the news would be better coming from Ally herself?

He paused outside the door, closed his eyes and issued yet another silent prayer. Then he pasted the closest thing to a smile he could muster onto his face and stepped into the room.

She was huddled beneath the covers in the fetal position. Her back was to him.

"Ally? It's me, Danny," he said softly.

She turned, her eyes red rimmed and puffy from weeping. The cheek he could see was streaked with tears. Noticing him, though, she smiled. "Oh, Danny, I need you so much," she whispered, awkwardly holding up her arms, though she was tethered by wires and tubes.

Danny raced to her and bent low over the safety rails to wrap her in his arms. "It's all right, Ally. It's all right. It's all right," he kept repeating as he attempted to gather her into his arms and hold her.

Who was he trying to convince, anyway? Ally or himself?

Ally lifted a hand and struggled to speak. "The baby—"

Danny pressed his fingers to Ally's lips. "It's all right, Ally. You don't have to talk about it. I know it's painful to lose our baby," he crooned, rocking her as best he could while he held her in his arms. "We can have other babies. I love you, and I want to be with you for always. That's all that matters. I want to be your husband."

Ally hugged him, too. Tears filled her eyes. She tried to blink them back, but they flowed unhindered, to be absorbed by the front of his uniform.

"Ally, you know I wanted the baby," Danny told her softly, struggling not to sound as choked up as he was. "But I want you so much more. I don't care if you make three times as much money than me. Hell, I'll stay home and be a house husband if that's what it takes for you to let me stay in your life this time. I don't care if you don't take my name. I'll even change my name to Carter if that's what you want. There are plenty of other Murpheys in this world. There's only one you.

"I love you, Ally. I can't imagine my life without you in it." He paused, and Ally put a finger to his lips to stop him, but he shook her hand away.

"I want us to be married, Ally. Before I leave for Tamahlyastan. If you'll have me," he added. He detached himself from her grasp and knelt on the ugly, linoleum floor. He cleared his throat. "Marry me, Ally. Please.

"I was going to give this to you tonight," he explained, extracting a small, velvet-covered jeweler's box from his pocket.

He opened the box and slipped the ring onto the trembling third finger of her left hand.

"Will you have me? Will you do me the honor of becoming my wife?"

Chapter Fifteen

Ally's heart swelled with gladness. She opened her lips to answer Danny's most eloquent proposal, but her heart seemed to have lodged in her throat. Tears still streaming down her cheeks, she nodded, then she shook her head, then nodded again.

"No?" Danny said, defeated. "I'll just go, then."

Ally had never heard him sound so beaten. Her heart broke.

"If you don't want me," Danny said, "I won't waste any more of your time."

He turned to go, but Ally grasped his sleeve. She was so tightly tethered that if he pulled away, she'd lose him, but it was enough. Danny faced her, the tension evident on his handsome face.

"What?"

"The baby," she finally managed to say around the enormous lump in her throat. "Still here."

His face lit up like a kid's on Christmas morning. "But you looked so sad. I thought—" He began to gather her into his arms, but the lines got in the way.

Ally stopped him by gently touching his hand. "Don't even think it," she whispered. "The baby is okay. Dr. Schmale had just come in and told me that she wasn't seriously harmed." She chuckled softly. "You've still got a lot to learn about women, I guess. These were tears of joy." Her eyes misted again just thinking about the doctor's good news. "I'll have to take it easy for a while, though.

"In fact," she added, "you'll like this part. I'll have to take a leave of absence from work until Danielle gets here."

At first the significance of the name seemed to go over his head, then Danny did a classic double take. "Danielle? As in Murphey?"

Ally grinned. "Absolutely. However, I will not saddle my daughter with Xaviera for a middle name. We'll have to do some negotiating on that."

"Hoo-ah," Danny cheered. "Anything you want," he agreed much too readily. "How about Carter?"

"Perfect. Danielle Carter Murphey," Ally said, testing the sound of the name. "I like it. It has a nice ring." She grinned again. "Of course, we still have to talk about what to tell Sweetie-Pie," she teased. "He's used to being the man of the house."

"*Bruiser* will get over it," Danny said, emphasizing the masculine name. "But I'm glad he's going to be there. He'll need to protect my girls while I'm gone."

"Yeah, right," Ally said. "If a burglar tries to break in, he'll lick him to death."

"Let's hope that there won't be any burglars," Danny said.

Ally nodded. "Hey," she told him. "You didn't even comment on the second part of my announcement."

"Second part of what announcement?" He stroked her hand, heavy with the weight of the gorgeous diamond ring.

"That I'm going to have to take a leave…"

"Ally," Danny said, holding her hand in his. "I've had a lot to think about the past couple of weeks. Not only about the baby, but about us and life in general.

"I don't give a damn how all the other Murphey men support their wives, I'm not them. If you want to work, go for it. Thinking about Lisa Hughes having to raise her son alone and not having the skills or the money to properly do it brought me to my senses, I guess. Besides, the rest of the Murphey men have nice, safe civilian jobs. They can pretty much count on dying in bed. I'm in a slightly more dangerous line of work."

Ally jerked her hand away from him. "Daniel Xavier Murphey. Don't you ever talk that way!" she said sharply.

"About what? Dying?" He shrugged. "It happens."

How could he be so cavalier about that? "Yes, but it had better not happen for a long, long time," Ally reminded him emphatically. "I have every intention of growing very old and wrinkled with you by my side."

Danny's face lit up, as if what she had been trying to tell him had just sunk in. "You know something? I asked you a question a little while ago. I'm not sure I actually got a straight answer."

Ally smiled. "What question was that?" she asked coyly. Of course she remembered full well what the question was, but how often did one woman get to hear it in her lifetime? It would be pure heaven to hear it again.

He took her hand and removed the ring.

"Hey, put that back," Ally demanded, grabbing at Danny's hand but in vain.

Danny held it up and away from her. "Not until I get my answer," he said. "Until then, you're wearing it under false pretenses."

"Heaven forbid," Ally said dryly. "By all means, ask away. However, I'm not sure I can guarantee you'll get the answer you're looking for."

"I'll get it," Danny said confidently.

He knelt again, and Ally loved him all the more for doing it. He cleared his throat and took her hand.

"Allison Raneea Carter, I love you with all my heart. Will you do me the great honor of becoming my wife?"

Ally smiled up at him, eyes once again streaming with tears. She nodded vigorously. Though her throat was still clogged with emotion, she managed to utter the most important sentence she'd probably ever say. "Yes, Daniel Xavier Murphey," she answered. "I would love to be your wife."

Danny's eyes looked a little moist, too, as he slipped the ring back on her finger, but that was just icing to make the moment all the sweeter. He held

Ally's hand and gazed down on her with such adoration that Ally's heart swelled again. How could life possibly get any better than this?

"Well, I guess congratulations are in order."

Unable to contain her joy, Ally peered beyond Danny to see Dr. Schmale standing in the doorway.

"Yes, they are, Dr. Schmale. This woman has made me the happiest man in the world," Danny said.

"No," Ally said. "He's made me the happiest woman."

Dr. Schmale smiled. "Now, now, this doesn't have to be a competition. It's wonderful news for both of you. However, I hate to be the bearer of bad tidings."

Danny's breath caught and Ally gasped. But Danny squeezed Ally's hand reassuringly as he voiced the question she was too afraid to ask.

"Is there something wrong with the baby?"

Ally had understood that the baby was going to be all right. What kind of bad news could the doctor possibly have?

The doctor shook her head. "I'm sorry. I didn't mean to worry you unnecessarily. Especially considering the day you've had." She turned to Ally. "You're fine. The baby's fine. I just don't want you getting overstimulated."

She turned to Danny. "You, Sergeant Husband-to-be, have to go. The woman needs to rest. You can spring her in the morning."

Danny faced the doctor and saluted. "Yes, sir, ma'am," he said cheerfully. Then he leaned over and gave Ally a peck on the lips. "You, I will see in the morning.

"We have some very important details to work out." He stepped toward the door.

"Yes, we do," Ally said. Then she remembered something. "Oh, no!" she exclaimed. "Sweetie-Pie. He's at home all alone."

"I told you not to keep calling him that," Danny said, feigning irritation. "It'll give him a complex."

Ally tried to sit. "Where's my purse? I need to give you my keys." How could she have forgotten all about her little Sweetie-Pie?

"Don't worry about a key, Ally. I'll take care of Bruiser," Danny said pointedly. "I can get into the house. It's one of those many skills I have that will never transfer to civilian life. At least not legal civilian life."

"Well, don't break anything," Ally said, feeling suddenly exhausted. "Oh, and when you get in, there's a letter on the kitchen counter from my aunt Myrtle. Looks like there'll be someone on the bride's side of the church after all."

Danny gave a thumbs-up, then strode out the door.

"He seems like a nice young man," Dr. Schmale noted as she felt Ally's pulse. "I suppose there's a story there."

"Yes," Ally said. "A long one. But it will definitely have a happy ending, and that's all that really matters."

"Well, you get some sleep now. You've still a little healing to do. And I'm assuming you have plans to make."

"That I do," Ally agreed through a yawn. "They can wait till tomorrow, though. It sure was nice that I finally ended up with my Sergeant for sale."

Clearly, the doctor didn't get her remark about the sale, but Ally didn't care. She was too tired to explain.

And blissfully happy.

HE DIDN'T LIKE TO MISUSE the covert skills he'd learned in special operations, but knowing how to pick a lock would come in handy now, Danny thought as he parked in Ally's drive and prepared to let himself in.

Ally's front door had a cheap, standard residential lock. He had no trouble getting in. However, neither would any half-witted burglar with a credit card. He would definitely have to change all the locks, and maybe look into getting a good alarm system put in before he left for overseas.

"Hey, Bruiser," he called, letting the puppy know that someone was in the house and coming to his rescue. Danny heard a series of resounding yips in reply. He chuckled to himself. "I have to give it to you, Bruiser. You got some lungs on you."

He crouched in front of the crate and released the latch. The puppy, tail wagging frantically, rushed out. "Hey, buddy, let's get you outside." He scooped the squirming puppy into his arms and carried him to the back door.

Danny stood in the kitchen doorway while the dog took care of his business. Finally, the puppy scampered up to him and tried to scramble up the back steps, distracting Danny from the envelope.

"Good job, buddy," Danny said, squatting to pet the dog, who rewarded him with a face full of wet, puppy kisses. He scooped the dog up, carried him inside and set him down next to the water bowl. "You have a drink, and I'll get your food."

Wondering what the guys in the squadron would think if they saw him talking to a dog, Danny reached for the bag of puppy food Ally had left out on the counter. An envelope on the counter caught his eye. "'Myrtle Carter,'" he said aloud.

Something about that name rang a bell. Not just the last name, Carter, but something else. He was pretty sure he'd heard it before.

If he could just remember where…

ALLY HAD BEEN GIVEN her release papers and she was impatiently waiting for Danny to arrive with a change of clothes and spring her. Finally free of the monitor and tubing, she sat in the chair by the window and tried to see outside. Wouldn't you know it. She actually had a view. Any other time, she'd be stuck with a front-row seat overlooking the parking lot.

She drummed her fingers restlessly against the plastic-covered arm of the chair. Why did good things always take forever?

The bad things always seemed to happen in an instant. Like her accident yesterday, she couldn't help thinking ruefully.

A nurse bustled in and sat on a chair near the bed. "Ready to go home?" she asked.

Ally nodded vigorously. "As soon as Danny gets here." She guessed she would have to depend on people to drive her around for a while, especially now that her own car was in Intensive Care.

"Do you have any questions?" the nurse asked.

Ally felt her face grow hot. She swallowed. "I…um. I…"

The nurse glanced toward the ring on Ally's hand. "You want to know whether you can have sex?"

"Yes, I'm getting married." Though it was policy not to keep valuables in hospital rooms, Ally had argued so bitterly with the night nurse who had tried to lock it up that she'd been allowed to keep it. Even if she had been required to sign a waiver. Ally didn't care. Nothing was going to keep her from wearing that ring. Nothing.

"Did Dr. Schmale tell you not to?"

Ally shook her head. "But then, I didn't ask," she added carefully.

"If she didn't say no, then I'd say yes," the nurse stated. She glanced down at the chart. "As far as I can tell from your chart, there's no medical reason not to. And since most pregnant people are married, doctors usually assume that relations will take place. So if she didn't specifically say no, I'd say go. Pregnant women are pretty resilient, though it doesn't hurt to be careful."

"Why am I not reassured?" Ally said.

"Every mother-to-be worries," the nurse said.

"And it doesn't help that you're going to be a bride, as well."

"I suppose," Ally said, feeling overwhelmed by everything she had to think about. This should be a happy time, full of plans and anticipation.

"Knock-knock," Kathie Palmore called from the doorway. "I'm sorry I wasn't here for you yesterday, but I didn't find out until the conference ended."

Ally was pleased to see her friend. Kathie was just the distraction Ally needed.

"I know you're going home this morning, but I thought I could help," Kathie said, stepping inside the room. "Do you want me to get anything for you? A change of clothes? Drive you home?"

"Got that all taken care of," Danny said from behind her.

Okay, so Ally might have been just a little partial to the man, but he had to be the most beautiful sight she'd ever seen. Though Danny was carrying her going-home clothes in her floral-patterned weekend case, he looked all man. He must have gone back to the Q and changed, because this morning he was wearing civvies. Still, he touched his forehead in deference to the colonel's rank.

"Thank you for offering," he said.

Colonel Palmore glanced back and forth from Ally, who couldn't stop smiling, to Danny, who appeared pretty pleased with himself, as well. "Do you know something I don't know?"

Ally held up her left hand, wiggling her fingers so that the diamond caught the light. No words were really necessary, which was a good thing. She got choked up every time she as much as thought of her little family-to-be.

Kathie understood immediately. "You are?" She turned to Danny. "Congratulations, Sergeant Murphey."

Danny beamed. "Yes, ma'am. I'm one lucky man."

"When?"

"Soon," Ally and Danny both answered in unison.

Ally laughed. "We haven't really set a date, but yesterday wouldn't be soon enough for me."

"Got that in one," Danny agreed. "Good news. I spoke to my C.O. this morning, and he's got me set up for emergency leave. I have another week here. Think that will be enough time?"

Kathie smiled and rubbed her hands with obvious glee. "Well, we might be able to throw a decent wedding together." She faced Ally. "What do you think?"

"All I want is a simple ceremony in a judge's chambers. How long does that take?" Ally said.

"Too long," Danny said.

"Hey, I've got good news. Remember that aunt you said you'd finally found?"

Ally nodded.

"I wasn't going to call her, but decided to after all. And guess what?"

"Danny, I'm an impatient woman," Ally said, smiling to show she wasn't upset with him. "I have a wedding to plan. And I do not have time to play guessing games."

"I know the woman. She's Patsy Prit—Patsy Darling's aunt, too."

Ally narrowed her eyes. "Why are you calling another woman 'darling,'? I don't like the sound of that."

Danny held up his hands for a time-out. "Hold on there. Darling is her last name. She married Ray Darling just a week or so before I got sent here. You know Ray, don't you? The one with the B.C. glasses who the guys call Radar?"

"No, that name doesn't ring a bell," she said, shaking her head. Surely she'd remember a man named Darling who wore those ugly government-issued glasses that the servicemen jokingly said were issued as a surefire form of birth control. She'd certainly have remembered a man called Radar.

"He got assigned to the squadron just about the time we…"

Ally understood why Danny didn't complete the sentence. She didn't like talking about it, either.

"Hey, hey," Kathie interrupted. "We have a wedding to plan. Look smart now," she said. "Danny, you go bring the car around."

"Yes, ma'am," he snapped, and executed a perfect salute.

"Ally, get dressed."

"Aye-aye, sir," Ally couldn't help teasing. She made a sloppy salute of her own.

DANNY STOOD QUIETLY in the chaplain's office off the chancel of the base chapel. How Colonel Palmore and Ally had managed to put this together so fast astounded him. But, he supposed, it was good to have friends in high places.

He tugged at the collar of his mess-dress uniform, brought from Florida by his best man, Second Lieutenant Ray Darling. He and Ray had been roommates until Ray had come back from Officer Candidate School. Then he'd married Patsy Pritchard, the woman "purchased by his aunt" for him in the same bachelor auction where Ally had bought Danny.

Damn, life was funny.

Neither Ray nor Danny had been real happy at being drafted to participate in that dog-and-pony show. But look how things had turned out. If this wasn't a happy ending, Danny didn't know what was. Even if he did have to wear this monkey suit again.

Ray slipped quietly into the office. "I just delivered Aunt Myrtle to the bride's room. I didn't try to see what was going on in there, but I think it's almost showtime."

Danny felt beads of sweat form on his forehead. He tugged at the collar again and fiddled with the bow tie that was a part of the formal mess dress. "It couldn't come too soon for me."

COLONEL KATHIE PALMORE, in her women's mess-dress uniform, helped Ally adjust her veil. Even puffed up like a giant silk-covered balloon, Ally couldn't help admiring her reflection in the mirror of the bride's room. There was something about the white organdy that made everything right.

The details of this wedding had come together so quickly that Ally almost wondered if she had dreamed everything. She wanted to pinch herself to make sure that wasn't the case, but on the other hand, if she did she just might wake up, and she sure didn't want that to happen.

A knock sounded on the door. Kathie let the veil fall around Ally's shoulders and went to answer. She opened the door a crack, lest it be Danny, who was forbidden to see the bride until the proper moment.

"Who is it?"

"I'm Myrtle Carter, the bride's aunt," a female voice, familiar to Ally after a week of phone conversations, replied.

Ally smiled in anticipation and spun around, eager to meet her newfound relative. The church was so stuffed with Murpheys she worried she might never learn all the names.

"Aunt Myrtle, I'm so happy to finally meet—" Ally stopped as she stared at the woman in the bright purple suit. Ally would recognize her anywhere. And she was still wearing a red hat, although this one was much more discreet than the other one. "Omigod!" she exclaimed. "I know you."

Aunt Myrtle and Kathie both looked puzzled.

"Well," Aunt Myrtle said slowly, "I guess we have gotten to know each other through our phone chats."

"No," Ally said, shaking her head. "We've met before. About six—no, seven—months ago," she said, automatically placing her hand on her tummy.

"I don't think so, dear," Aunt Myrtle said, shaking her coiffed gray head.

"Yes. We did. You're the lady who had the extra ticket to the bachelor auction. You were wearing a red hat and a different purple outfit. How could I possibly forget that? If you hadn't given me that extra ticket you had and I hadn't gone to the auction, I would never have 'bought' Danny. And I wouldn't have been getting ready for a wedding today."

"Almost like a fairy godmother," Kathie said, echoing what Ally was thinking.

"Well, dear, I do remember that, now that you've reminded me," she said, seeming to muse out loud. "What an odd turn of events. Who would have thought that our paths could have crossed like that and we didn't realize it."

"And to think that I had lived for several years in the same county and never knew you were there." Ally chuckled. "It's funny. I realized I might have some family on my father's side, but I really didn't consider trying to find anyone until I discovered little Danielle was on the way."

"Well, my dear, you have another cousin you've yet to meet. My niece, Patsy Darling, is married to the best man. You'll get to meet them both at the reception."

Aunt Myrtle glanced at Ally's swollen tummy, evident beneath the cream-colored peau de soie. "However, if I really were a fairy godmother with magical powers, one would think I'd have timed things better."

Ally smiled at her aunt. She might only have just met the woman, but it seemed as though they'd known each other forever. Maybe there had been some sort of cosmic connection that had made them cross paths before the auction.

Whatever the reason, Ally thought happily as she heard the organist begin to play the "Wedding March," everything had worked out for the best. Today, she was a princess, fairy godmother and all.

And she was about to wed her handsome Prince Charming.

Could anything but a very happy ending be far behind?

Epilogue

Danny paced the delivery room waiting area like the impatient father-to-be he was. Danielle wasn't supposed to make her appearance in the world for another couple of weeks, but she'd decided that tonight, the evening before her daddy was to depart for his assignment in Tamahlyastan, was the perfect moment to come into the world.

As far as Danny was concerned, his daughter's timing was impeccable.

Danny had wanted very much to participate in the birth, but because he and Ally weren't expecting him to be in the country, they'd agreed that Colonel Palmore would attend the prenatal classes and act as Ally's coach. Now Danny was feeling more than a little excluded.

"Congratulations, Sergeant. You're a dad," a masked-and-gowned figure, obviously Colonel Palmore, announced from the doorway. "Your wife is ready to introduce her daughter to her daddy. They're waiting for you."

This was the moment he'd been waiting for. He paused only long enough to give Colonel Palmore a bear hug.

Danny still had a hard time calling the colonel by her first name, but he would have to get used to doing it. The woman was Ally's best friend, and he'd already been promised an assignment at headquarters when he returned from his overseas tour. So he'd be seeing the woman on a regular basis.

"Is she…? Are they…?"

"Wife and daughter are just fine," the colonel said. "Go," she said, shooing him with her hands. "Don't keep them waiting. After all, that precious little girl had to work hard to get here early so she could see her daddy off."

Danny didn't miss the glint of tears in the colonel's eyes.

"Go on," she said gruffly. "Time's a-wastin'."

"You don't have to tell me twice," Danny said, hurrying down the hall.

A smiling nurse pointed him toward the recovery room. "Congratulations, Daddy."

Danny just beamed. Everything had happened so quickly that he hadn't had a chance to buy cigars. He guessed he would owe everyone, but even those would have to wait until he returned from his tour.

He paused in the indicated doorway and drank in the sight of mother and child. His wife. His child. He couldn't have painted a more perfect picture if he'd been an old master painting the Madonna and Child. "Beautiful" was all he could manage to say.

Ally looked up, tired, but smiling through happy tears. "Oh, Danny, I never knew I could love anyone so very, very much," she whispered, stroking the baby's dark, fuzzy head.

"Me, either," he said huskily as he sank to his knees beside the bed. He touched the thick fuzz. "So soft," he said with wonder. "But so beautiful. Just like her mother."

"She has her daddy's curly hair, though," Ally said, allowing one tendril to curl around her finger. She looked at her husband, tears of joy spilling from her eyes. "I love you both."

"Yeah," he said thickly. "I love you, too. And I'll do everything I can to make this tour of duty pass as fast as possible so I can get back to make a family with you both."

"No," Ally said. "With the three of us. You forgot…Buddy."

Danny had to smile. "You're right. There will be three of you keeping the home fires burning—you, Danielle and Buddy, the dog. A guy couldn't dream up a better happy ending if he tried."

* * * * *

Welcome to the world of American Romance!
Turn the page for excerpts from
our June 2005 titles.

BELONGING TO BANDERA
by Tina Leonard

THE MOMMY WISH
by Pamela Browning

AN ENGAGEMENT OF CONVENIENCE
by Mollie Molay

SARAH'S GUIDE TO LIFE,
LOVE & GARDENING
by Connie Lane

We hope you enjoy every one of these books!

Tina Leonard continues her popular Cowboys by the Dozen series with *Belonging to Bandera* (#1069). These books are wonderfully entertaining, fast-paced and exciting. If you've never read Tina Leonard, you're in for a treat. After all, who can resist a cowboy—let alone twelve of them! Watch for the tenth book, *Crockett's Seduction,* coming in September 2005.

Meet the brothers of Malfunction Junction and let the roundup of those Jefferson bad boys begin!

Bandera looked out the window as he and his brother, Mason, drove by the miles of their ranch. "We have one pretty spread of land. I'm going to miss Malfunction Junction."

"We're only going to be gone a few days," Mason said.

"Well, I like my little corner of the world just the way it is," Bandera said. "Hey, look at that!"

Bandera craned his head to look at the woman on

the side of the road, waving a large sign. She was wearing blue-jean shorts and a white halter top. "Probably a car wash," he murmured. "Slow down, Mason."

"No," Mason said. "There's no time. This is going to be an information-seeking venture, not a woman-hunt. Nor do I need a car wash."

They whizzed past so fast Bandera could barely read her sign. The blonde flashed it at him, holding it up high, so that he got a dizzying look at her jiggling breasts, white teeth, laughing blue eyes and legs. She was so cute, he was sure the fanny she was packing was just as sweet. "Stop!" he yelled.

"No!" Mason said, stomping on the brake anyway. "Why couldn't you have stayed home?"

"Her sign says she needs assistance," Bandera said righteously, although he really thought it had read *I'm Holly*.

"And Lord only knows we never leave a lady without assistance." Mason glanced up into his mirror. "I sense trouble in a big way."

The lady bounced to Mason's truck door. "Hi," she said.

"Howdy," Mason and Bandera said together. "Can we help you, miss?" Bandera asked.

"I'm waiting for my cousin," she said.

Mason was silent. Bandera took off his hat. "Did your car break down, miss?"

"No." She smiled, and dimples as cute as baby lima beans appeared in her cheeks. Bandera felt his heart go *boom!*

"I'm getting picked up by my cousin," she said. "That's why my sign says *I'm Holly.*"

"Nowhere on her bright white placard do I see the word *assistance,* Bandera. Or even *Help!*" Mason sent his brother a disgusted grimace.

"We haven't seen each other in a while," Holly said. "He might not recognize me."

"Okay," Mason said. "You'll have to pardon us. We need to be getting along. Normally, we don't stop for ladies holding signs, but we thought you needed help."

"Actually, I do," she said. "I could use a kiss."

Bandera's jaw dropped. "A kiss? Why?"

"I'm feeling dangerous," she explained, "Since I just caught my fiancé in bed with my best friend."

"Ouch," Mason said.

"Precisely. That's why I called my cousin. This is our prearranged meeting place."

"So you're running away," Mason said.

"I'm going on a well-needed sabbatical," she corrected him. "We were getting married tomorrow. I don't feel like hanging around for the tears. I have an itch to see the countryside."

"Actually, you have an itch to get as far away from your fiancé as possible," Mason theorized.

"You understand me totally."

"So about that kiss…" Bandera began, unable to resist.

This month, look for Pamela Browning's *The Mommy Wish* (#1070), from our Fatherhood series. As always, this author offers us a wonderful setting for this warm romance. A single father, his seven-year-old daughter and our heroine are temporarily stranded in the small town of Greensea Springs. In this unique Florida community, Molly Kate McBryde finds herself becoming attached to Eric Norvald's little girl…and to Eric.

Rain again. Cold and dreary, beating against the wide window of the great gray skyscraper housing the McBryde Industries corporate offices. And on the console in front of the window, a framed picture of Molly Kate McBryde and her grandfather, taken in a more salubrious climate, before she'd started this miserable job in this miserable building that always seemed engulfed in miserable weather.

"Your grandpa Emmett called," chirped her assistant, the cheery and irrepressible Mrs. Lorraine Brinkle of the short blond curls and flippy skirts.

Molly tossed her briefcase on the antique rolltop desk that had once been Emmett's. "I'd better call him back. How did he sound?"

"You know. Like always, and with that Irish brogue of his. Flirting shamelessly. Teasing me about wanting your job."

Molly grinned. "On days like today, you can have it. So much responsibility, so little time." She was Number-Two Honcho in Corporate Accounting, a position that had its trying moments.

"I didn't mean that the way it sounded," Mrs. Brinkle amended. "Anyway, I'm looking into a promotion to Legal."

Molly felt a prickle of apprehension. She didn't want to lose Lorraine Brinkle, a woman of many skills. Mrs. Brinkle had not only worked a stint as a legal secretary before she'd signed on at McBryde Industries, but she'd also been trained as a bookkeeper. On top of that, she had attended college at night for years before graduating with a degree in business six weeks ago at the age of forty-five.

"Oh, don't threaten me with Legal. We need you here," Molly said hastily.

"Mmm-hmm. But now that I've got my college degree, I'm ready for bigger and better things. That's what your grandfather says, anyway." Mrs. Brinkle rolled her eyes.

"What else did he say?"

"Only to call him," Mrs. Brinkle said. She

scooped a stack of file folders off Molly's desk and winked. "He mentioned something about sending you to Florida."

Florida sounded like a good idea. This was the last week in October, and whitecaps were scuffing the chill gray surface of Lake Michigan, and this morning, Molly had discovered moth holes in last year's winter coat. She picked up the phone.

Her grandfather answered on the first ring. "Molly Kate," he said before she could say hello. "I want you and Patrick to sail *Fiona* to Fort Lauderdale."

"Um, Grandpa," Molly said. "I have a job. You hired me."

"How long ago was that? Seven years? Isn't it time you had a vacation?"

"I came to Maine this summer. We took *Fiona* to Nova Scotia, remember? A good time was had by all."

"Well, now *Fiona*'s getting refurbished and repaired in North Carolina. I can't take her to Florida myself because I'm having some medical tests."

"Tests?" Molly said, alarmed. Since their Nova Scotia voyage, Emmett had suffered a few spells of dizziness, which, considering his heart condition, was alarming, but she'd thought everything was under control now that he was on medications.

"Oh, you know how it is. Doctors like to help out other doctors, so they're sending me to Minneapolis, where a new team of doctors will probably send me to some more doctors."

"Grandpa, you're scaring me."

"I hope I can scare off those doctors, as well. I want the boat in Florida when I get there, though."

"If I run off on this junket to Florida, who's going to look after things here?"

"Why, Mrs. Brinkle, of course. She's a go-getter, that one."

He was right. And keeping Lorraine Brinkle busy in Corporate Accounting would prevent her from pursuing an alternate destiny in the Legal Department until they could figure out some way to promote her to a job more in keeping with her many capabilities.

"I'll need to square it with Frank." Francis X. O'Toole was her boss, head of the department.

"I've already talked with him. You go with his blessing."

"Don't you think you should have let me broach the idea? Don't you think you're a bit too presumptuous, Grandpa dear?"

"Don't you think *you* protest too much, Molly dear?" Her grandfather's tone was teasing.

Molly sighed. "When do you want me to leave?"

"It'll most likely be the first of the week."

"Who's going to be my crew?"

"You are. I've hired a licensed captain who can help you get the boat to Fort Lauderdale."

"Who is it?"

"Never mind. Just…someone."

"A happy relationship requires that a woman make her man feel masculine…" And so begin the six rules created by sociologist Lucas Sullivan, who believes following these rules will lead to a happy marriage. But Lucas revised his "theory" after meeting April Morgan in *Marriage in Six Easy Lessons* (#1023) and now his best friend must as well! In the final book of the Sullivan Rules series, *An Engagement of Convenience* (#1071), Tom Eldridge learns that no relationship can be boiled down to rules—especially one with the spirited and sexy Lili Soulé. After all, these rules never said anything about women with two unruly young children….

"So, you're the one!"

At the sound of her boss's angry voice, Lili Soulé tried to cover the damning evidence in front of her. But it was too late to cover the draft of a flier demanding the management of the Riverview Building keep its child-care center open.

To add to her alarm, the charcoal sketch she'd been idly drawing was left in full view. If she wasn't already in trouble over her latest flier, she would be in deep trouble now.

Two years of working for Tom Eldridge, the publisher of *Today's World* magazine, where she worked as a graphic artist, hadn't diminished the crush she had on him. She'd been too shy to show it, but at moments like this the sound of his full baritone made her fingers ache to draw him, as she was caught doing now.

He was a man who took great pains to avoid socializing with his staff. He'd sounded friendly enough at weekly staff meetings, but he sure didn't sound friendly now.

Lili's heart raced as she turned to meet Tom's gaze. He was six feet of rugged masculinity, with a square jaw and, at the moment, angry chocolate-brown eyes. Heaven help her, he was grimly regarding her work on the drafting table. The frown that creased his forehead and the glow of fire in his eyes weren't helping Lili hold on to her courage. Still, now that her identity as the building's rabble-rouser was out in the open, she intended to put up a good defense. She nodded cautiously.

"So, you're the person who's been circulating fliers and a petition to keep the building's day-care center open?"

"Yes," Lili replied, shaking slightly. "Someone has to do it."

"And, of course," he added wryly, "that someone had to be you?"

Lili didn't like the way Eldridge was looking at her, but the damage was done. If ever there was a time to assert herself and her right to free speech, that time was now. It was also time to forget how he unknowingly affected her.

"Yes. I have twins in after-school care. Someone had to do something to help convince the building's management to keep from closing the center," she added in a defiant voice that not only seemed to surprise him, it surprised her, too.

Her boss's eyes narrowed. He pointed to the assignment sheet pinned to the corner of her drawing board. "I would have thought you'd be spending your time working on your assignment instead of spending your time stirring up trouble."

She gestured to a large sheet of drawing paper under the damning flier. "I started to, but another thought or two got in the way."

Eldridge motioned to the flier. "Yeah," he agreed grimly, "it sure looks as if something did get in the way. Like causing problems for everyone, including me."

Lili didn't intend to back off. The center had provided tender, loving care for her twins for two years before they'd reached first grade. Now that the twins were in after-school care, keeping the center open became more important than ever. She had to live with her conscience.

To Lili's dismay, he reached over and picked up the charcoal drawing she'd been working on. "What's this supposed to be? A wall target for you to shoot at?"

Lili wished she could fade into the woodwork. She was a mature woman, a single mother with twins, she told herself. Only an infatuated teenager drew pictures of a man who had captured her interest as this man had captured hers.

"No. I heard the sound of your voice and started drawing…" How could she tell Tom he was seldom far from her thoughts without sounding like a love-struck idiot?

Sarah's Guide to Life, Love & Gardening (#1072) is Connie Lane's third story to take place at the very romantic Cupid's Hideaway. If you had a chance to read *Stranded at Cupid's Hideaway* (#932) or *Christmas at Cupid's Hideaway* (#996) you'll remember some of the residents of South Bass Island, like the delightful Maisie, proprietor of the inn, and police chief Dylan O'Connell. If not, you'll enjoy meeting them for the first time—as Sarah does.

Connie Lane is a multi-published author who writes with genuine charm and humor. But there's wisdom that accompanies the wit, and characters who'll find a place in your heart. By the end of the book, you'll wish Cupid's Hideaway was a real place!

What is romance?
It's the question that Affairs of the Heart *viewers ask most often.*
Is romance about a look? A touch? Is it something

as simple as the scent of lilacs wafting through an open doorway? Ah, if only it were as easy as that! But don't despair, dear reader. You have Sarah's Guide to Life, Love & Gardening. *And Sarah has all the answers.*

—Sarah's Guide to Life, Love & Gardening

"…until then, this is Sarah Allcroft of *Affairs of the Heart,* wishing you beauty-filled days, elegant nights and a lifetime of romance."

Sarah held the smile. One second. Two seconds. Three.

"Cut!" Gino Felice, her director, gave her the thumbs-up and Sarah released the breath she was holding, along with the smile that cramped her face muscles and left her lips as dry as dust. Gino hurried over to where she was perched on a white wicker settee artfully accessorized with a dozen chintz pillows in a variety of colors and patterns. Flowers and checks, stripes and watercolor splashes, they all complemented her blush-pink linen suit to perfection. Sarah wouldn't have it any other way.

Gino kissed her cheek. "Gorgeous, darling. Your best show ever. One look at the tea you set this afternoon…" There was an assortment of adorable little canapés, finger sandwiches and cookies on a silver tray on the table in front of Sarah. Gino reached around the Limoges teapot and cups they'd borrowed from a local collector for the taping and grabbed a sandwich cut in the shape of a star. He popped the blackberry, sage and cream cheese concoction into his mouth, closed his eyes and smiled while he chewed.

"As soon as they see this episode, the good folks over at the Home & Hearth Network will jump up and take notice," he said. "They're going to want you in the fall lineup. I'd bet my silver-haired granny on it. I wouldn't be surprised if the phone started ringing with offers. Very soon."

Sarah wouldn't be surprised, either. Then again, there was little that ever surprised Sarah. She simply wouldn't allow it.

Her determination settled in the place that always felt jumpy before, during and after every taping and like it always did, it calmed Sarah and filled her with confidence.

By the time Becky Landis raced by to answer the phone that was ringing in the outer office, Sarah was smiling again.

"Good show, honey!" Becky was the producer, makeup artist and wardrobe mistress of *Affairs of the Heart.* She was also Sarah's best friend. She patted Sarah on the back as she zoomed by. "You got the directions for those knitted sachet bags, right?" she called over her shoulder. "I know we're going to get slammed by requests. Like we always do. And it's going to get crazier once we go national!" The last Sarah saw of her, an ear-to-ear grin was brightening Becky's expression.

Sarah knew exactly why. Once *Affairs of the Heart* was picked up for cable, she wasn't the only one whose star would rise. Becky would finally get the chance to work on a network show, just as she'd always dreamed. Gino and the rest of the crew would have the opportunity, at last, to use their considerable talents on a project more challenging than a shoe-string-budget show with a tiny local audience.

Sarah, however, was the only one who was going to get thrust, pushed, dragged and swept into the limelight.

Her smile wilted and her insides started jumping all over again.

One more taping out of the way.

One more bullet dodged.

Again.

She wondered how long she could keep it up.

HARLEQUIN®

AMERICAN *Romance*®

Catch the latest story in the bestselling
miniseries by

Tina Leonard

Cowboys BY
THE DOZEN!

When Holly Henshaw, wedding planner
extraordinaire, ended up alone at the altar, she
decided then and there: no more true love.
Adventure, excitement, freedom—that's what she
wanted. Then she met Bandera Jefferson. The
cowboy was ornery, possessive…and sexy as the
dickens. Now, wild-at-heart Holly has begun to
think she just might like belonging to Bandera.

BELONGING TO BANDERA

Harlequin American Romance #1069

Available June 2005.

And don't miss—

CROCKETT'S SEDUCTION

Harlequin American Romance #1083

Coming in September 2005.

www.eHarlequin.com   HARBELBAN

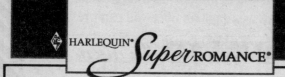

HARLEQUIN *Super*ROMANCE®

They're definitely not two of a kind!

Twins

His Real Father
by **Debra Salonen**
(Harlequin Superromance #1279)

Lisa never had trouble telling the Kelly brothers
apart. Even though they were twins, they were
nothing alike. Joe was quiet and Patrick was the
life of the party. Each was important to her.
But only one was the father of her son.

Watch for it in June 2005.

Available wherever Harlequin Superromance books are sold.

www.eHarlequin.com   HSRHRF0605

If you enjoyed what you just read,
then we've got an offer you can't resist!

Take 2 bestselling love stories FREE!

Plus get a FREE surprise gift!

Clip this page and mail it to Harlequin Reader Service®

IN U.S.A.	IN CANADA
3010 Walden Ave.	P.O. Box 609
P.O. Box 1867	Fort Erie, Ontario
Buffalo, N.Y. 14240-1867	L2A 5X3

YES! Please send me 2 free Harlequin American Romance® novels and my free surprise gift. After receiving them, if I don't wish to receive anymore, I can return the shipping statement marked cancel. If I don't cancel, I will receive 4 brand-new novels every month, before they're available in stores! In the U.S.A., bill me at the bargain price of $4.24 plus 25¢ shipping & handling per book and applicable sales tax, if any*. In Canada, bill me at the bargain price of $4.99 plus 25¢ shipping & handling per book and applicable taxes**. That's the complete price and a savings of at least 10% off the cover prices—what a great deal! I understand that accepting the 2 free books and gift places me under no obligation ever to buy any books. I can always return a shipment and cancel at any time. Even if I never buy another book from Harlequin, the 2 free books and gift are mine to keep forever.

154 HDN DZ7S
354 HDN DZ7T

Name	(PLEASE PRINT)	
Address	Apt.#	
City	State/Prov.	Zip/Postal Code

Not valid to current Harlequin American Romance® subscribers.

Want to try two free books from another series?
Call 1-800-873-8635 or visit www.morefreebooks.com.

* Terms and prices subject to change without notice. Sales tax applicable in N.Y.
** Canadian residents will be charged applicable provincial taxes and GST.
All orders subject to approval. Offer limited to one per household.
® are registered trademarks owned and used by the trademark owner and or its licensee.

AMER04R   ©2004 Harlequin Enterprises Limited

eHARLEQUIN.com

The Ultimate Destination for Women's Fiction

For **FREE online reading,** visit
www.eHarlequin.com now and enjoy:

Online Reads
Read **Daily** and **Weekly** chapters from
our Internet-exclusive stories by your
favorite authors.

Interactive Novels
Cast your vote to help decide how these
stories unfold…then stay tuned!

Quick Reads
For shorter romantic reads, try our
collection of Poems, Toasts, & More!

Online Read Library
Miss one of our online reads?
Come here to catch up!

Reading Groups
Discuss, share and rave with other
community members!

For great reading online,
visit www.eHarlequin.com today!

INTONL04R

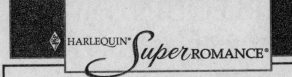

HARLEQUIN *Super* ROMANCE®

COLD CASES: L.A.

A *new mystery/suspense miniseries from*

Linda Style,

**author of The Witness
and The Man in the Photograph**

His Case, Her Child
(Superromance #1281)

He's a by-the-book detective determined to find his
niece's missing child. She's a youth advocate equally
determined to protect the abandoned boy in her charge.
Together, Rico Santini and Macy Capshaw form an uneasy
alliance to investigate the child's past and, in the process,
unearth a black-market adoption ring at a shelter for
unwed mothers. The same shelter where years earlier
Macy had given birth to a stillborn son. At least,
that's what she was told....

Available in June 2005 wherever Harlequin books are sold.

www.eHarlequin.com

HSRHCHC0605

HARLEQUIN *Super*ROMANCE®

Stranger in Town
by
brenda novak
(Superromance #1278)

Read the latest installment in Brenda Novak's series about the people of Dundee, Idaho: STRANGER IN TOWN.

Gabe Holbrook isn't really a stranger, but he might as well be. After the accident—caused by Hannah Russell—he's been a wheelchair-bound recluse. Now Hannah's in his life again…and she's trying to force him to live again.

Critically acclaimed novelist Brenda Novak brings you another memorable and emotionally engaging story. Come home to Dundee—or come and visit, if you haven't been there before!

Available in June 2005 wherever Harlequin books are sold.

www.eHarlequin.com

HSRNOVAK0605